SAINT - THE BUCK BOYS HEROES SERIES

DEBORAH BLADON

FIRST ORIGINAL EDITION, 2022

Copyright © 2022 by Deborah Bladon

All rights reserved. No parts of this book may be reproduced in any form or by any means without written consent from the author.

This is a work of fiction. Names, characters, places and incidents either are the product of the author's imagination or are used fictitiously. Any resemblance to actual person's, living or dead, events, or locales are entirely coincidental.

eBook ISBN: 9781926440705
ISBN: 9798835915972

Book & cover design by Wolf & Eagle Media

deborahbladon.com

CHAPTER ONE

CALLIE

"WAIT!" I yell as I race out of my apartment with one of my red-soled heels in my hand. "Hold the elevator!"

I slam the door shut before turning to face the open elevator at the end of the corridor.

Just as I suspect, my gorgeous neighbor is standing front and center in the elevator with a smirk on his face as he tugs his phone out of the inner pocket of his suit jacket.

Dammit.

He's all perfectly styled dark brown hair, big brown eyes, and a body that I can't stare at too long or all kinds of dirty fantasies trample every other thought I've ever had.

The man is the epitome of hot, but he's rude.

He's not just rude. He's next level extra rude.

"Hold it," I call out. "I'm going to be late for a job interview unless I get on it now."

The smug-faced jerk raises his big hand in the air and

waves at me like he's on a float in a parade as the elevator doors slide shut.

"Asshole!" I scream just before they close, hoping this time he gets the message that he's not a good neighbor.

He's the worst neighbor I've ever had, and that's saying a lot.

Until a few weeks ago, I lived in a cramped two-bedroom walk-up with three friends from college.

Our next-door neighbor was our landlord.

He never had one complaint about any of us, but he must have wished he were a chef in another life because every night, he'd cook up something that smelled like a sewer.

He always brought the leftovers over to our place.

Not wanting to insult him, one of us would accept the food with a grin.

Even if we sprinted down to the basement to toss it in the incinerator as soon as the coast was clear, the lingering scent of his home-cooked meal permeated our apartment until the next night when the same thing happened again.

That's one of the reasons why I jumped at the opportunity to stay at my oldest brother's apartment while he's working in Phoenix for three months.

When Grady asked if I'd apartment sit to help him out, I knew that he was doing it as a favor to me.

Living rent-free in a luxury apartment in a building on Madison Avenue is a step up in every conceivable way.

Or it was until I realized that I live next door to one of Manhattan's biggest jerks.

I glance to the left when I hear a door creak open.

"Calliope?" The woman who lives down the hall from me peeks out from around her partially open apartment door. "Is everything all right, dear?"

When we first met in the lobby, I introduced myself as

Callie Morrow. She took it upon herself to ask if that was short for Calliope. Not wanting to start off on the wrong foot, I decided not to lie, so I admitted that was my name.

She hasn't stopped calling me that since.

"Everything is fine, Mrs. Sweeney," I call out to her. "I have a job interview, and I missed the elevator."

"You can take the stairs," she suggests.

I'm all for that, but we're on the twenty-second floor, and I'm wearing a snug skirt. "I'll wait for the elevator."

I trudge past her, still holding tightly to my left shoe. I finally shimmy my foot into it once I'm at the elevator. I push the call button twice. Once to send it sailing back up here as soon as Mr. Big Jerk gets off in the lobby, and a second time while pretending I'm poking him in the eye.

If Mrs. Sweeney didn't have her eagle eyes on me, I'd be partaking in a round of boxing with the air at the moment to ease all of the pent-up frustration I feel.

She ventures out of her apartment far enough to give me a view of her lilac tracksuit and matching sneakers. It pairs perfectly with the gray curls on her head.

Mrs. Sweeney's fashion sense is on point.

When I'm eighty-nine, I hope I look as fabulous as she does.

She gives me a look from head to toe, pushing her wire-rimmed glasses up the bridge of her nose. "That outfit you're wearing screams professional woman looking for a full-time, high-paying job with benefits and room for advancement, Calliope."

That's saying a lot.

I chose a black pencil skirt and plain white blouse because it's what every female executive at Mirnan Mortgage wears. I did a deep dive on their social media pages last night to get a feel for the company.

It's not my dream job, but bartending won't fulfill all of my financial goals.

That's my current gig since I lost my junior marketing position with a party supplies company when a competitor bought them out.

I've worked at the bar on and off for the past three years since I turned twenty-one. When I found myself without a job last month, the bar's owner offered me two extra shifts per week. I'm grateful, but I have a degree in marketing that I want to put to use.

Mrs. Sweeney skims a hand across her left cheek. "Fix your hair there."

I'll take the critique because I know she wants the best for me. I push a few strands of my dark brown hair behind my ear. "How's that?"

"You're a beautiful blue-eyed girl." She sighs. "You remind me of myself sixty-five years ago."

Just as I'm about to comment that she's as stunning now as she was in the black and white photographs she has shown me, the elevator dings to signal its arrival on our floor.

"Wish me luck."

"You don't need luck," she says matter-of-factly. "You have experience and ambition. You're one of the smartest women in this city."

"From your lips to Mr. Mirnan's ears." I laugh.

As soon as the elevator doors slide open, I step into the car and turn to face her. "I'll see you later, Mrs. Sweeney."

"Knock them dead, Calliope."

CHAPTER TWO

Callie

MRS. SWEENEY IS some sort of sorceress, or bad luck is trailing me like a lost puppy.

I stand on the sidewalk outside the Greenwich Village office of Mirnan Mortgage and watch as a body in a bag is wheeled past me on a stretcher.

Mrs. Sweeney told me to knock them dead, and that's what happened.

Technically, I didn't knock Mr. Mirnan dead. I didn't even see him. When I arrived for my interview, an ambulance and police cars were already here.

The receptionist I had spoken to yesterday when I booked my interview was sobbing as she sat on the curb.

It seems Mr. Mirnan was having breakfast when he keeled over onto his desk.

By the time the EMTs arrived, he was already gone.

"The job isn't available anymore," the sad-eyed receptionist calls out to me. "Mr. Mirnan always said when he dies, the company goes with him."

A few of the mortgage brokerage firm's employees turn to look at her.

I take a breath and make my way to where she's sitting. "I work at a bar a few blocks from here. Do you need a drink?"

Her tear-filled brown eyes look me over. "It's not even ten a.m. yet."

I'd tell her it's five o'clock somewhere, but there's no need to cast that lure in her direction. She's already bouncing up to her feet. "I could use a strong martini."

"I make a killer one," I say before I wince.

Dammit, Callie. Inappropriate, much?

A slow smile creeps over her lips. "Mr. Mirnan would have laughed at that. He always laughed at my lame jokes."

I take the backhanded compliment with a smile of my own.

"We can walk to the bar." I point to the corner. "The drink is on me."

Her gaze wanders to where her co-workers are all huddled together. "I'm sorry the job didn't work out for you, Callie."

I shrug a shoulder. "It wasn't meant to be."

"I'm Jade." Her hand snakes toward me. "Jade Mirnan."

I take her hand in mine and perk an eyebrow before following up with the obvious question. "Were you related to him?"

I don't motion toward the back of the van where the body bag is being placed, but Jade puts two and two together when she looks at it. "He's my husband's uncle. He insisted I call him Mr. Mirnan at work and during family get-togethers. All the time, really."

I would say that I'm glad I won't be working for him

because it sounds like he was a pretentious ass, but Jade doesn't need to hear that while she's grieving.

"I'll be right back. I'm going to grab my purse," she says through a sniffle. "Thanks for the free drink offer, Callie. You showed up at just the right time."

I take one last look at the van as a man dressed in a black suit slams the doors shut.

There goes my latest job opportunity.

With any luck, my next interview will go a hell of a lot better than this.

―――――

"DO I want to know why you and our only customer are dressed like twins?" My boss, Gage Burke, shoots me a smile from across the bar.

I laugh.

I arrived at Tin Anchor with Jade over an hour ago.

Since the bar wasn't officially open yet, I used my key to unlock the door.

Gage greeted us immediately and didn't balk when I said I would cover the cost of Jade's martini before I prepared it.

I know Gage well enough to know he doesn't expect me to pay for it.

He's generous to a fault. He's that way with all his employees, including my older brother, Zeke, who works here part-time as he pursues a career in computer animation.

"Jade works at the office where I was supposed to have an interview this morning," I explain quietly. "Or worked at, I guess."

Gage leans closer to lower his voice. "She was fired?"

I steal a glance at where she's sitting next to a round table near one of the windows overlooking the sidewalk. "Her boss died this morning."

Gage's green eyes widen. "That's brutal."

I nod. "I saw them bring the body out. It was horrible. Jade worked for her husband's uncle, so his death hit her hard."

We both look in her direction to find her dragging her hands through her short blonde hair.

"Make her another martini," Gage says. "On the house."

I look at him. "You're sure?"

He smiles. "She looks like she could use it, and I could use a favor."

I've asked dozens of favors of Gage over the past few years, and he's granted all of them. I respond without thought. "Tell me what you need."

"I know you weren't scheduled to work today, but Katie wants to meet up for lunch." A warm smile accompanies his wife's name. "Can you cover for me for a couple of hours at noon?"

"Consider it done."

"Thanks, Callie." He pats my hand. "The right job will come along soon. I know it's not a lot, but if you can cover another extra shift every week, it's yours."

"You know how much I appreciate that, right?" I ask.

"I know." He glances at Jade again. "Set her up with another drink, and thanks again for stepping in to help."

It's the least I can do, and besides, the mid-day crowd usually consists of corporate types that work high-powered jobs. I'll walk out of here with a fist full of tips that will go directly toward my one and only debt.

Maybe this day won't be a total loss after all.

CHAPTER THREE

Callie

"WELLS IS HIRING," Jade announces with a glance in my direction. "They're looking for an administrative assistant, and there's a position in marketing too. You know Wells, right?"

She follows that up with a giggle and a wink.

She's on her third martini.

I wouldn't classify her as tipsy, but she's feeling less pain than when we arrived three hours ago.

I asked if she wanted me to call anyone for her, but she told me that she had already sent a text message to her husband asking him to stop by here after his lunch meeting.

I look to the two tables that are now occupied.

I served up their drinks quickly while keeping an eye on Jade.

In an abstract way, I feel responsible for her.

That's not a burden, but it is a distraction.

I stand next to her and nod. "I know that company."

"They have that enormous billboard in the middle of Times Square." She laughs. "Every time I pass it, I take a minute to appreciate the man in the picture, including what's inside his underwear. It's obvious he's got a lot to work with."

I glance down at the floor.

It's impossible to miss that billboard.

It's an image of a man from the neck down. The Wells name is stitched in red lettering across the gray waistband of the white boxer briefs the model is wearing.

The man in the image is sporting a noticeable bulge.

It's not as though I've stopped to stare, but I know some women have.

I've witnessed that myself.

I shift the subject because I'd rather talk about a potential job than what's in a random model's underwear. "Are you going to apply for the administrative job?"

Her head snaps up. "Me? No. Why would you think that?"

Let me count the reasons.

She lost her job today due to the untimely death of her boss. Her phone's browser is opened to a job listing website, and not more than thirty minutes ago, she was sobbing into her martini about how badly she needs a job.

I don't touch any of that because she goes on, "I'm looking for a job in the field I was trained in. My job at Mirnan Mortgage was never going to be forever. I want to get back to doing what I love, and I think now is the perfect time."

The question begs to be asked, so I do it. "What field were you trained in?"

She looks me in the eye. "I'm a high-wire performer."

I stare at her because I need time to process that.

Fortunately, the sound of the bar's door opening and muted male voices save me from continuing this conversation at the moment.

I turn to greet my newest customers, but I freeze as soon as I spot the man leading the pack of three into the bar.

Goddamn this day all to hell.

Out of all of the bars in Manhattan, why did he have to walk into mine?

My annoying neighbor smirks when he catches sight of me wearing a black bib apron.

I yanked it from behind the bar and put it on so I wouldn't stain my white blouse with an unwanted splash of anything.

The apron is available for any employee's use whenever citrus needs to be cut, or vegetables have to be cleaned for garnishes.

Normally, I'm dressed in jeans and a T-shirt when I'm working here.

The gorgeous jerk in the suit stalks toward me, raking me from head to toe as he does.

His eyes land on the apron. "Congratulations are in order, Champ. It looks like you got the job after all."

Champ.

The name is stitched in white thread on the apron. I found it at a vintage store called Past Over a few months ago. I picked it up when I was looking for sundresses. I knew the apron would come in handy at work, so I paid a couple of dollars for it and brought it straight here.

"Sit yourself," I say curtly to my neighbor.

"Will do." He motions to the two men with him to head to an empty table in the corner. "Three glasses of scotch. Neat. The best label you have."

"Scotch," I repeat. "One for each of you."

"You got it," he says in a deep voice that sends a charge straight through me. "Keep up the good work, Champ."

When he brushes past me to take a seat at the table, I roll my eyes.

Working for one of the world's most prominent men's underwear brands wasn't on my radar, but as soon as Gage returns, I'm going to apply for the marketing position at Wells.

Seeing my neighbor here is a sign.

It's a sign that I need to find a job that will keep me as far out of his orbit as possible.

"THANKS FOR THE DRINK, SAINT!" A male voice calls out, startling me.

I turn just in time to see my neighbor pop his middle finger in the air. That's directed at one of the men leaving the bar. He follows that up with a hearty, "fuck you, Decky."

I'd expect to hear this exchange late on a Saturday night when a bunch of college-aged guys wander in, but these men are both dressed in well-tailored suits and are wearing shoes that cost a small fortune.

I should know.

I worked part-time for a few years at a high-end shoe store.

The third of their trio chuckles as he exits the bar behind Decky.

My neighbor is on his second glass of scotch, and although he's a generous tipper, I'm ready for him to take off too.

I glance at the watch on my wrist.

"Champ!"

Rolling my eyes, I look over at my neighbor again. I raise my chin in a silent query.

He curls one of his index fingers to lure me over.

Great.

Since Jade left fifteen minutes ago, I've been tending to the other few customers in the bar while working on polishing my resume on my phone.

I thought it was as good as it could be, but since I want that job at Wells, I need to put my best foot forward.

I round the bar and approach the man who has barely taken his eyes off me since he arrived.

As soon as I'm near his table, he's out of his chair and on his feet.

He towers above me, but that's not saying a lot. I'm barely five foot one, and I've only gained three inches with these heels.

The brute in the suit in front of me is at least a foot taller than me.

"We've lived next door to each other for how long now?" he quizzes me.

Twenty-seven days is the correct answer, but I shrug. "A few weeks, I guess."

It feels much longer.

My neighbor from hell is notorious for listening to music late at night. I asked Mrs. Sweeney if it kept her awake too, but she pointed at her hearing aid and giggled.

The guy also loves inviting people over. It's not just women. Whenever a baseball game is on TV, he's wearing a jersey.

How do I know that?

The peephole in my apartment door is a perfect method of surveillance.

I've seen him in the hall outside my apartment dressed in

that jersey and jeans as he greets his loud-mouthed friends as they exit the elevator.

Then, I'm subjected to three hours of whistling, yelling, and cursing when the game doesn't go the way they want.

The man standing in front of me may be blessed with gorgeous looks, but he's lacking in common courtesy DNA.

"Now that I know your name, Champ, don't you think it's time you know mine?"

"I know your name," I snap back. "It's Saint, right?"

He lets out a throaty laugh that sends goose bumps trailing up my arms.

Why is his laugh so sexy?

"My asshole brother is the only person who still calls me that." He rubs his beard-covered jaw. "It's a nickname from when I was a kid."

"You must have been a lot different when you were a kid, Saint. I can think of at least a dozen nicknames that suit you better."

His gaze passes over me from head to toe. "Like what?"

"You don't want to know."

His left eyebrow perks. "I sure as hell do, Champ."

Seriously? Are we having this discussion right now?

"For starters, I'd call you a horrible neighbor," I say with exasperation edging my tone.

A smirk slides over his lips. "How am I a horrible neighbor?"

"I don't have time for this." I glance at my watch. "I need to get back to work."

"Fine." He tilts his head to the side. "Get me another drink."

"Another one?" I ask before I realize the question has left my lips.

I don't need him to hang out here any longer. I want him out of this bar now.

"Is that a problem?" he questions.

"Don't you have a job to get back to?" I paste on a sugary sweet smile. "I wouldn't want your boss getting pissed at you for taking too long of a lunch break."

"That's not going to happen," he says. "You're not denying me another beverage, are you?"

I am, and it's not because he's intoxicated. It's because he's annoying the hell out of me.

I point at his empty glass. "You downed two drinks pretty fast today. I know how much you like scotch, but maybe save the next one for when you're at home tonight. You indulge a lot during the evenings and weekends. I've seen that for myself."

"You what?" He takes a half step closer to me. "When did you see that? Have you been spying on me?"

Yes, but I'll never admit it.

"I've seen it two times." I dart two fingers in the air. "Twice, you've knocked on my door when you've had a drink in your hand."

A smile slides over his lips. "Right."

He doesn't add anything else even though both times that happened, I asked what he wanted, and he said he needed to borrow a cup of sugar.

I told him to get lost. He did after he smirked and winked at me.

I look at my watch again. "I need to get back to my other customers. Have a nice day."

"Have a nice day?" His arms cross his chest. "Telling your customers to stop drinking is not the way to hold onto this job, Champ. Ever heard of upselling?"

There's no way in hell he thinks that Champ is my actual

name, but I won't correct him.

As soon as Grady is back in Manhattan, I'll find a new place to live, and I'll never have to see this guy again.

"My job is none of your business," I snap, mimicking his stance.

"I'm back!"

Relief flows through me when I hear Gage's voice behind me.

"My boss is here," I say before I turn around.

Gage is grinning when I spot him. "Sorry that took so long."

I rush toward him. "It's not a problem at all."

"Did everything run smoothly?" Gage asks that question every time he steps away from the bar.

"Smooth as silk." I smile. "If it's all right, I'm going to take off. I have a lead on a job I think I'm perfect for. I want to apply today."

"Go." He grins. "If they have any sense, they'll hire you."

I move around the bar, rid myself of the apron, and grab my purse and phone. "That's exactly what I'm hoping for. I'll be in tomorrow night for my shift. I won't leave you short-handed."

"You're the best," he says as he glances around the bar. "Is everyone settled up, or…"

I look to the left and then the right, taking an extra second to lock eyes with my neighbor.

"Everyone is squared away."

"Perfect." Gage sighs. "You're a lifesaver. If you need a solid reference, point your potential new employer in my direction."

I may just do that.

I want that job at Wells more than I've wanted anything in a very long time.

CHAPTER FOUR

Callie

"DO you have any experience in men's underwear, Callie?"

I've put my hands in a few pairs while they were on men I was about to go to bed with, but I don't think that's what the marketing manager for Wells wants to know.

Shaking my head, I smile. "I've worked in retail settings, and I've held marketing positions, so I think I bring a solid, well-rounded experience to Wells."

I'd pat myself on the back for that answer if I could. It's a ten out of ten.

I've been in prep mode since I got the call two days ago that I'd landed an interview with Wells. I didn't want to walk into this unprepared, so I wrote down every answer to the questions I anticipated may be asked of me.

The woman interviewing me grins. "I see that you worked at Polleys for a time. I love that store."

I do too.

When I worked at the shoe store part-time in college, I used most of my earnings to buy designer shoes. My employee discount was fifty percent, so I viewed each purchase as an investment in my future since I knew I'd wear them to a corporate job one day.

"Polleys was a great foundation for me," I explain. "I spent almost all of my time with customers. That gave me a clear understanding of what they were looking for and what appealed to them in terms of our marketing endeavors. I helped the owner create a very successful digital marketing plan."

I worked at the independently run shoe store when they had one location. They've branched out to two now. I can't take credit for that, but the owner was more than happy to listen to my ideas when it came to marketing.

Delora, the woman interviewing me, leans forward. "Your experience in digital marketing makes you an ideal candidate for the job. We have a strong presence online, but we want to expand. We're looking for someone to join our team who has fresh ideas and experience to back that up."

"I believe I possess all of that," I say with confidence.

I did launch a statewide campaign for the party supplies company, but it never reached its full potential. The company's owner was near retirement age and decided to sell out to a competitor who already had a full staff in place.

"I have a few more candidates to meet with," she says softly. "I'll call you by the end of the week to let you know."

I've had enough interviews recently to know that although it doesn't qualify as a brush-off, it's not a job offer either.

I move to stand. "Thank you for your time."

She looks up from where she's sitting behind her glass

desk. "Thanks for coming in, Callie. Maybe I'll see you again soon."

Or maybe not.

AN HOUR LATER, I step off the elevator and pause because I spot Mrs. Sweeney on her tiptoes with her face mere inches from my apartment door.

From this angle, it almost looks like she's trying to see into my apartment through the peephole, but it doesn't work that way.

I know because I tried that myself once to make sure that my annoying neighbor couldn't see in.

It was after he'd pounded on my door one Saturday afternoon. I wasn't in the mood for his sugar-borrowing antics, so I never opened the door.

I did peer through the peephole as he was knocking incessantly. The sight that greeted me sent me stumbling back a few steps. He had one of his eyes pressed against the peephole.

It was both alluring and alarming. I felt as though I was in the middle of a horror movie where the villain is literally drop-dead gorgeous.

The sound of my heels clicking on the floor lures Mrs. Sweeney's gaze in my direction. A blush settles over her cheeks as she steps back from my door.

"Calliope," she calls out as I approach her. "You look like you just came from another job interview."

My gaze skims her face before it lands on what looks like a yellow sticky note on my door. "I did."

On any other day, she'd be asking me twenty questions about the potential job, but today that's not happening. She glances at the sticky note. "It looks like someone left a message for you."

I move around her to pluck the note from the door before I read the masculine handwriting.

If you want a lesson in upselling, you know where to find me.

"IS THAT FROM A FRIEND OF YOURS?" Mrs. Sweeney asks in a tentative tone.

"No," I answer honestly. "An enemy."

A nervous laugh stutters out of her. "You know what they say about keeping your enemies close."

"I think it's more important to keep friends close," I say, noticing the pink tracksuit she's wearing and the sneakers on her feet. "Do you want to go for a walk in Central Park? I can change my clothes in no time flat."

I'm dying to get out of this blue pencil skirt and matching blouse. My feet are screaming for a break from the three-inch heels I'm wearing.

Her face lights up. "I'll never turn down an opportunity to get some fresh air."

"I'll be ready in ten minutes," I tell her as I unlock my door. "Do you want to come in and wait for me?"

"Meet me in the lobby when you're ready," she calls out as she heads toward her apartment. "I'm going to get my secret weapon in case we run into your enemy."

I glance over my shoulder. "What's your secret weapon?"

"I carry a mini air horn in my fanny pack." She winks. "I haven't had to use it yet, but a girl should always be prepared."

Laughing, I duck into my apartment, grateful that at least one of my neighbors is a sweet soul.

CHAPTER FIVE

CALLIE

PATIENCE MAY BE A VIRTUE, but it's also a living hell when you're waiting to hear back from multiple companies while searching for a new job.

Not only did I interview with Wells last week, but I met with the owner of a small tech firm. She was looking to launch her company's first marketing campaign, and two days ago, I sat down with the human resources manager of a string of hotels.

My patience has finally paid off because an hour ago, Delora called to offer me the job at Wells.

She ran through all that is required of me, including signing an employment contract and filling out various forms. When she asked if I could start three days from now on Monday, I answered with a resounding yes.

Since I was set to see my older sister today, I suggested that we meet in Times Square so I could share the good news with her.

I know she'll get a kick out of the larger-than-life billboard of the underwear model.

"That's the company I'm going to be working for." I point at the billboard. "Wells is my new employer."

"Do you think there's a sock in there, or is it all him?"

My head snaps to the right to catch sight of my sister's face. She's smiling as she stares up at the billboard.

"What did you just say?" I ask her, trying to suppress a laugh.

Naomi shoots me a look. "I asked if you think that underwear model has a sock in those boxer briefs or if that bulge is one hundred percent all him?"

I point at the stroller right in front of her. Her hands are resting on the handle. The plain gold band circling her ring finger seems brighter in the late afternoon sun. "Tabitha is right there. Do you want her to go home and tell Harlan that you're drooling over some random model's package?"

She leans closer to me. "It's his dick, Callie. It's not hard to say."

She follows that up with a high-pitched giggle.

Shaking my head, I peek at her three-year-old daughter, who is thankfully fast asleep with her head resting on the soft blanket in the stroller.

"That was a penis pun," Naomi points out. "I thought it was a great one. Hard. Dick. Get it?"

I sigh.

"Oh, wait." She levels a finger in my face. "You haven't gotten any in months, have you? When's the last time you have sex, Calliope?"

"As if I'm going to tell you." I smile. "You don't need to know when I have sex, and I don't want to know when you do."

"It's pretty obvious that I'm getting some." She squeezes

the handle of the stroller. "I have two kids already, and this one on the way means Harlan is still delivering in the bedroom."

I glance at her swollen belly under the pink sundress she's wearing. "You're five months along now, right?"

She slides a hand over her stomach. "Give or take."

Looking into her blue eyes, I smile. "That baby is lucky to have you as a mom."

"I know it," she says with a curt nod. "I am killing it as a mom if I do say so myself."

Wrapping an arm around her shoulder, I laugh. "I say so too."

Her gaze wanders back to the billboard that showcases a man's ripped torso and a pair of white boxer briefs. "What do you think his face looks like? I lucked out when I married Harlan because he's as beautiful as he is built."

I turn my attention to the billboard. The model posing with his hands on his hips has abs for days. He may look like utter perfection, but I'd guess a hell of a lot of airbrushing went into creating that image. "Who knows? Maybe what we're looking at is all he has going for him."

"Doubtful," she blurts. "Since you'll be working there, you're bound to meet him, right? Take a selfie with him so I can put a face to all of that."

Laughing, I shake my head. "I don't think I'll meet him. I have a junior position in their marketing department, Naomi. I doubt I get direct access to models."

"You'll make it happen," she says with confidence edging her tone. "If I didn't love being at home with my kids so much, I'd be envious of you and your new job."

I glance at the stroller. "You have the best job in the world."

"I really do," she agrees with a smile. "I'm starving. Do

you have time for an early dinner? It's my treat. Harlan is taking Bodhi to baseball practice, so it's boy's night. They'll grab some pizza on the way home. You know how much Bodhi loves pizza."

I do know. My seven-year-old nephew can eat half a cheese pie by himself.

I look down at the white blouse and denim cut-off shorts I'm wearing. Wherever we go, it's going to have to be casual.

"Let's go to Lise," she suggests. "They have that salmon quiche there that the baby adores."

She's the one who adores it, but I'm in. I'm not picky when it comes to food, and the bistro she loves has excellent food and service.

Naomi steals one last glance at the billboard. "Goodbye, Callie's future husband."

I bark out a laugh. "Never in a million years."

"Never say never," she tosses her favorite quote at me. "You can't predict what the future holds."

I smile as I hear Tabitha stirring in the stroller. "I can predict that you will have a very hungry little girl on your hands in the next ten seconds. Let's get to Lise."

CHAPTER SIX

CALLIE

I GLANCE at the clock on my nightstand before I scream into my pillow.

It's ten minutes to two.

In the freaking morning.

I'm due to start my new job at Wells in just seven hours.

I haven't got a wink of sleep yet because my neighbor has been partying hard since nine o'clock. I was hopeful that it would quiet down as it usually does at around midnight, but the volume ticked up then.

More people arrived.

My jerk of a neighbor went out in the corridor to greet them. I watched all of it through my peephole as my blood boiled.

Swinging my legs over the side of the king-sized bed, I step onto the hardwood floor.

There is enough light filtering in through the window that

I can make out where I dropped my faded jeans and sweater on a chair near the closet.

I march over and slip them on before raking a hand through my hair.

I don't care if I look horrible.

I'm dead tired, annoyed, and aching to scream at my neighbor.

I shove my feet into the first pair of shoes I find, stumbling briefly because three inch red heels aren't the best choice, but I'm too tired to scrounge around in the dimly lit room to find something more appropriate.

I march through the apartment toward the foyer, stopping briefly to scoop up my keys before opening the door.

The sight that greets me is enough to send me back into my apartment.

A man and a woman are making out as they wait for the elevator. His hand is sliding beneath the skirt of her dress.

"No shame," I mutter as I approach the door to Saint's apartment.

I knock once and wait, knowing it's unlikely anyone will answer.

The music drowns out everything, including the muted voices that I hear behind the door.

I curl my hand into a fist and pound on the door. I do it repeatedly, hoping by some miracle that someone inside will hear the noise and open the door.

It works.

The door swings open, and he's there.

Dressed in jeans, a light blue button-down shirt, and expensive wingtip shoes, my neighbor cocks a brow. "Hey, Champ."

My gaze drops to the glass in his hand. Unsurprisingly, it's filled with amber liquid. "Shut the party down, Saint."

That sends his head back in raucous laughter.

I glance past him to catch sight of dozens of people in his apartment.

What the hell?

Don't these people have jobs to go to in the morning?

"I'm not kidding," I say. "I can't sleep. Your music is too loud. There are way too many people. Are you breaking the building's fire code?"

Apparently, he finds that just as amusing because he chuckles with a shake of his head. "It's not that loud. You need to lighten up. Let me make you a drink."

He can't be serious?

My arms cross my chest. "I don't want a drink. I want your party to be over."

A woman behind him screams just as something crashes to the floor.

His gaze darts over his shoulder. "The party is just getting started."

"The party needs to be over, or I'm calling the police," I threaten even though I know the NYPD isn't going to rush over here for a noise complaint.

His brown eyes widen. "You're bullshitting me, right?"

Exasperated, I stomp my foot on the floor. "Tomorrow is an important day for me. I need to get some sleep."

He leans his shoulder against the doorjamb as the party rages behind him. "A drink will help you sleep. Name your poison. Are you a red wine drinker, or do you prefer beer? I've got both and more."

I swear his gaze drops to the front of his jeans.

Another crash echoes through the apartment as the noise seeps into the hall.

I can't believe that even without her hearing aids, Mrs. Sweeney can sleep through this. What about the people that live above and below this man? This has to be pissing them off too.

"I don't want a drink," I stress. "Shut your party down now."

He shakes his head as he sips from the glass in his hand. "Not happening, Champ."

Frustrated, I stare into his eyes. "You're the asshole brother, aren't you? Decky is probably the good brother."

That pulls more laughter from him. His entire broad chest shakes. "Decky is a dick. I'll introduce you. He's doing shots in the kitchen."

Livid, I spin on my heel and march back toward my apartment door.

"Don't go, Champ," he calls after me. "I promise you'll have fun if you come inside."

I turn and offer him my middle finger.

He presses his fingertips to his lips, kisses them, and then pretends to blow that kiss to me.

"Jerk," I mutter under my breath as I open the door to my apartment.

I don't look back again before I shut it and head to my bedroom to get my phone.

CHAPTER SEVEN

CALLIE

"YOU'RE BELLIGERENT," a uniformed NYPD officer says to my neighbor an hour later. "I cuffed you for my safety and yours."

Saint shakes his head. "I assure you that you're safe with me."

The officer's gaze trails the spots of blood that dot the corridor leading from Saint's apartment door to the elevator. "It looks to me like someone isn't safe."

My neighbor shoots a look at me. "What exactly did you say when you called them? They think I fucking murdered someone."

"Did you?" The officer asks him. "You have a few blood spots on your shirt too."

"Jesus Christ," Saint groans. "Someone had a bleeding nose. I tried helping her, but she took off."

The officer pulls a notepad out from her belt. "I'm going

to need to ask you a few questions. We can do that at the station or in your apartment. Your choice."

"My apartment?"

She nods. "Unless there's something in there that you don't want us to see?"

A few more people trail out of his apartment. A steady stream of partygoers has left since the police arrived ten minutes ago.

"Like what?" Saint snaps back. "A dead body?"

I've watched enough episodes of Dateline to know that's not the correct answer.

Another officer stalks toward where I'm standing just outside of my apartment. He was the one who knocked on my door when they first arrived. "If we need anything more from you, we'll let you know. Have a good night."

I glance at the time display on my phone.

It's the middle of the night, but if I crawl into bed now, I'll get at least a couple of hours of solid sleep.

"Thank you," I say with a smile. "I appreciate this."

A rough sigh leaves Saint. "I don't."

The female officer shoots him a look. "The sooner we talk, the sooner we'll get all of this sorted out."

I take one last look at my neighbor with his hands cuffed behind his back.

I had no idea it would come to this, but from what the officer said to me when they first arrived, I wasn't the only one in the building who made a noise complaint.

Maybe next time the inconsiderate jerk has people over, he'll think twice about partying into the wee hours of the morning.

WHEN I HAD my interview at Wells last week, I was too nervous to appreciate the beauty of their offices.

They inhabit the top three floors of a building in lower Manhattan.

I took the subway to work because I wanted to time the commute. Fortunately, I arrived twenty minutes early, so I had time to grab a small coffee at the café in the lobby of the building. Tomorrow, I can give myself an extra few minutes at home before I bolt out the door.

I scan the reception area of Wells, marveling at the modern style. The walls are painted white and decorated with abstract paintings.

My gaze shifts to the polished concrete floors and the curved reception desk. It looks like it's crafted from recycled wooden boards. The blonde-haired woman sitting behind it is dressed in red.

Wells has mastered the sleek and sophisticated look.

Before applying for the job, I quickly scanned the company's website to familiarize myself with the brand.

It was thin on details about the founders or anyone currently holding a corporate position.

The site was focused on their products and how they believe they are superior to other comparable brands.

The woman behind the reception desk glides to her feet and waves at me. "Callie, right? Delora told me to expect you."

I approach her with steady even steps even though my knees are quaking.

Part of that is from first day nerves. The other part is from pure exhaustion.

As I was getting dressed today in a simple navy blue skirt and a white blouse, I had my eyes closed. When I popped them open, I realized I had incorrectly buttoned the blouse. It wasn't surprising, given that I only snuck in two hours of sleep thanks to my asshole neighbor.

"I'm Dionne." The receptionist smiles. "Delora is in a meeting, so Mr. Wells is on his way down to greet you."

"Mr. Wells?" I question.

"He's one of the owners of the company," she explains, her voice quieter than it was. "His bark is worse than his bite. Don't let him intimidate you."

I swallow past a sudden lump in my throat.

I had a hard-ass boss at the party supplies company, and even though I handled him with ease, it didn't make for the best work environment.

I glance over my shoulder when I hear footsteps approaching behind me. A handsome brown-haired man in a dark blue suit walks toward me.

He looks vaguely familiar to me.

"Good morning, Mr. Wells," Dionne greets him. "How was your weekend, sir?"

"Fine." He offers her a nod of his chin as he hurries past me.

As soon as he disappears around a corner, Dionne glances at me. "That's not the Mr. Wells you'll be meeting with. That was his older brother."

Silently nodding, I try and place that man's face.

I've seen him before.

Millions of men live in New York City, so I must have passed him on the street at some point.

"Here comes the other Mr. Wells." Dionne plants both elbows on the reception desk as she leans forward. "It's go time, Callie."

I suck in a deep breath and turn slowly to face my new boss.

Shit. Double shit.

Standing five feet from me, wearing a tailored gray suit, a black button-down shirt, and a matching tie, is my neighbor.

"Saint?" I question under my breath.

He adjusts one of his stunning silver cufflinks as he rakes me from head to toe. A sexy smile slides over his lips. "You're the new hire?"

With my stomach tied in nervous knots, I nod. "I am."

"Follow me, Champ. We need to talk."

CHAPTER EIGHT

Sean

I MIGHT FIND this situation laughable if I wasn't so fucking tired.

Who am I kidding?

This is goddamn hilarious.

The woman who called the police on me last night works for me.

Champ is trailing me as I greet my executive assistant before heading straight into my office.

I would have confronted her on the elevator ride up here from reception, but it was jam-packed with employees. They each had something to say to me. Most were a cheery, '*good morning.*' Some used the confined space to compliment me on my tie or suit.

I don't know if they're fishing for a raise, but since I don't know most of them by name, their good intentions aren't going to result in any type of advantage.

My brother is the one they should be directing their

niceties to. He knows everything about every fucking person who works here. He not only addresses all of our employees by name, but he also knows every birthday and hire date.

I head toward my desk and flip open the file folder that Delora Green, the head of our marketing department, shoved at me before she raced into a meeting.

Giving new hires a company tour and standing by their side as they sign their employment contracts is not my job.

It's not Delora's either, but our human resources manager is out sick today, so the task of acquainting our newest employee with the company has fallen on my shoulders.

I planned to hand this off to someone else after meeting the person at the reception desk, but then I saw who it was.

Champ, my beautiful neighbor and the woman who had me detained by the police last night, is now an employee of mine.

Fate can be such a sweet beast.

"Mr. Wells," she says from where she's standing. "I had absolutely no idea that you owned this company."

Curling a finger in the air, I lure her closer. "Take a seat."

She hesitates before settling her ass in one of the two chairs facing my desk.

Her legs cross and then uncross.

It would seem that someone with a sharp tongue and full pink-stained lips is nervous as hell.

I glance down at her employment file.

Calliope Morrow.

She earned an MBA at New York University.

Her experience in marketing is limited, but her references are impeccable.

If I had a hand in the hiring process, I wouldn't have signed off on this, but my brother has the last say in that department.

As COO, he handles most of the mundane tasks because of his detail-oriented brain.

I'm the CEO because I drew the longer straw.

I literally drew the longest drinking straw out of the fist of a friend in the parking lot of a fast food place the night my brother, and I conceived the idea to launch this company.

A knock on the doorjamb sends my gaze from Calliope's tanned legs to my older brother's face.

"Declan," I say sternly *because why the fuck is he even here?*

"Declan," Calliope whispers under her breath. "Decky."

Watching her piece things together is entertaining as hell.

"Sean, you need..." Declan's voice trails as he glances at the back of Calliope's head. "Are you in the middle of something?"

Her gaze drifts over her shoulder to him.

His blue eyes narrow. "Have we met?"

I don't need him and his handsome as fuck face to get involved in this, so I try to shoo him away. "I am in the middle of something."

Declan ignores that and steps into my office. "I swear I've seen you before."

"I was at the reception desk when you walked past earlier," Calliope explains. "Maybe that's where you know me from."

If she's trying to hide the fact that she works at a bar, she's wasting her time.

I don't care what our employees do on their own time, and I sure as hell know Declan will look past it as long as it doesn't impact her performance here.

"That's not it," he presses, shooting her a megawatt smile complete with dimples.

Fuck him.

He taps his index finger against his chin as he studies her face. "You work at that bar. Tin Anchor, and… wait. Are you the woman who called the police on Sean last night? You're his neighbor. I swear I saw you talking to one of the officers."

Calliope's gaze snaps back to me.

I see a plea in her eyes followed by a flash of resignation.

"I didn't know," she whispers. "I had no idea that he owns the company. If I knew, I wouldn't have called…"

"Co-owns the company," Declan corrects her as he approaches her chair. "What exactly are you doing here?"

"She's our new marketing hire," I tell him. "This is Calliope Morrow."

He lets out a low chuckle. "I'll be damned. Things just got a hell of a lot more interesting around here. Welcome aboard, Calliope."

Her hand moves to take the one he's offering.

She gives it a firm shake. Envy shoots through me as she gazes up at my older brother's face.

This is all I fucking need.

I have a goddamn crush on our new employee. It would have to be the one woman in Manhattan who hates me.

"I'm excited to get to work," she says with excitement edging her tone.

"I'll handle Calliope's introduction to the company," Declan directs that at me. "There's an issue with a shipment dropped off at reception by mistake. Why don't you go deal with that?"

Why don't you go to hell, Decky?

I keep that to myself as I storm out of my office.

How will I handle working with this woman when she can't fucking stand me?

CHAPTER NINE

Callie

I SIGN on the dotted line that guarantees my employment with Wells unless I mess up.

It seems that calling the police on one of the co-owners of the company isn't enough to warrant termination.

I'm grateful.

The salary is substantial enough that I'll have no problem affording rent on a modest studio apartment after Grady returns to Manhattan in a couple of months.

The benefits package is amazing too.

On paper, this is the best job I've ever had.

Declan drops his gaze to my signature as he slides my employment contract toward him. "It looks like you're all set."

I nod. "I'm excited to get started, sir."

He looks beyond my shoulder to the open door of his office. "You'll be reporting to Delora directly. She's been here from day one and has a firm understanding of what we're looking for in terms of our vision for marketing our brand. It was her rousing recommendation that landed you this job."

I make a mental note to thank her for that when I see her.

He shoves my employment contract into a manila folder labeled with my name. "It's quite a coincidence that you live next door to my brother."

I manage a stilted laugh. "It's temporary. My brother owns that apartment. I'm housesitting for him until he returns to New York."

"I apologize for my part in what happened last night." He leans back in his leather office chair. "I wasn't aware that you were bothered to the point that you felt it necessary to call the police on Sean."

Sean.

Saint.

Whatever we call him, he's still my annoying neighbor, but now he's also one of my bosses, so I need to tread carefully.

I take a deep breath. "It was difficult to sleep with all the noise, and I wanted to be at my peak for my first day here."

I won't apologize for how I handled things. I did what I felt I needed to at the moment. I couldn't have anticipated that Sean would end up in handcuffs.

"Understood." He pushes back from his desk to stand. "I'll walk you to the marketing department, so that you can get acquainted with your new co-workers."

That's another positive sign that this Mr. Wells is willing to overlook what happened last night.

I follow on his heel as he steps out of his office.

"Declan." The deep baritone of Sean's voice fills the air. "You're needed in accounting. I'll take over from here."

My head turns to the left in unison with Declan's as Sean approaches us.

Declan glances back at me. "If you run into any issues, Delora will always be around for you. We're happy to have you on board, Calliope."

Not wanting to continue being called that, I gently correct him. "I go by Callie. I prefer it over Calliope."

"Callie it is," he says.

Sean pats him on the shoulder. "Get to accounting, Declan. People are waiting on you."

"Right." He turns his attention to his brother. "I'm having lunch brought in for us. Be in my office at one, so we can go over projections for next quarter."

"Yes, sir." Sean laughs.

Shaking his head, Declan chuckles as he walks away.

Sean looks at me. "All right, Calliope. You're about to get the grand tour of Wells. Try and keep up."

"It's Callie," I say as I fall in step beside him as he takes off toward the bank of elevators.

His focus stays straight ahead. "I prefer Calliope."

"I don't," I counter.

He looks down at me as he slows to a stop before stabbing a finger into the elevator call button. "We expect a hell of a lot from every one of our employees. My brother is a hard-ass when it comes to the small details. That means you need to be on time every day. You start work at nine. Your workday ends at six. My driver has my car at the curb in front of our building at precisely eight forty every morning. Starting tomorrow, we ride to the office together."

Stunned, I follow him onto the elevator when the doors open. "What? I take the subway to work."

"Not anymore." He presses the button for the floor below us. "I've seen how disorganized you are in the mornings,

Champ. Be on the sidewalk in front of our building by eight forty, and I'll get you here on time. You're welcome."

"I didn't say thank you," I mutter.

As the doors start to slide shut, he chuckles. "You will."

I don't ask what the hell that means because I feel as though I'm caught between a dream and a nightmare.

This job is everything I could have wanted, but the man standing next to me is at the very least partially responsible for my future with this company.

I have to get along with him if I want to hold onto this job.

Right now, that feels like an impossible task.

CHAPTER TEN

SEAN

"I'M IMPRESSED, SEAN."

I don't hear those words every day.

I turn to see my brother enter his office. As expected, he shuts the door behind him.

I've already helped myself to one of the two meatball sandwiches tempting me from a paper bag on his desk.

He knows what I like.

These sandwiches, complete with the sodas on the side, capture one of the best memories from when we were kids.

We grew up surrounded by wealth. Our grandfather on our mother's side was one of the wealthiest men in the country.

Our father was just as fortunate. Even though he had a trust fund, he worked his way through college so he could land a job at one of the city's museums as a curator. His parents scoffed at the choice, but my dad loves art, and that job was his dream.

He'd take Declan and me to a diner for lunch every Saturday. Meatball sandwiches and sodas were always on the menu. All we had to do was finish our portion and agree not to tell our mom what we had for lunch.

She didn't approve of the menu choice or the diner.

To her, a casual lunch has always been a minimum of three courses.

Watching my brother unwrap his sandwich, I swallow before chasing the food down with a sip of cola. "Impressed? How so?"

He casts me a look. "Seriously? You don't know?"

I can't read his goddamn mind, and he knows that, so I widen my eyes. "Toss me a clue, Decky. Are you impressed with the projections for next quarter? You know that the billboard in Times Square has a lot to do with our uptick in revenue."

He rolls his eyes. "It has nothing to do with it."

I huff out a laugh. "Sore loser."

"Bastard," he says before taking a sizable bite of the sandwich.

Scratching my chin, I sip from my can of soda. "I know. You're impressed that I convinced the police to let me go last night. That was masterful, if I do say so myself."

He swallows hard. "They let you go ten minutes after I left because I told them they had no grounds to hold you."

Declan likes to flaunt his law degree whenever the opportunity strikes, but he bailed on me while I was still cuffed.

"Most lawyers would wait around until their clients are cleared before they leave with a random woman."

His eyebrows shoot up. "You're not a client. You're my brother, and for the record, I left alone, Sean. I knew they were going to release you. It's no big deal."

He's right about that. It wasn't a big deal and certainly not the first time I've been handcuffed.

"I'm impressed that you didn't rescind the job offer to Callie Morrow once you realized who she was." He sets his sandwich down. "That's a mature move."

"My personal issues with her aren't relevant to her job."

That piques my brother's interest enough that he leans forward in his chair. "You have personal issues with her that reach beyond her having you arrested?"

"No." I shake my head. "She's my neighbor. She called in a noise complaint. Pulling the job offer because of that is petty."

"Listen to you." He points a finger at me. "You sound like a reasonable, responsible business owner."

I take another bite of my sandwich to refrain from calling him a dick.

"It only took thirty years for you to get to this point." He chuckles.

"My thirtieth birthday isn't for another six months, old man." I smirk.

"Old man?" he snaps. "I've only got three years on you, Saint."

Shaking my head, I pick up the soda can. "I'll ignore that for now. Let's talk sales numbers. I have a meeting in midtown in an hour."

"Fine." He wipes his hands on a paper napkin before turning his attention to his laptop. "Your projections are solid, Sean, but I know we can do better. I want us to come up with something fresh for the winter campaign. Maybe Miss Morrow will have something new to add to the marketing team's vision."

She might.

Only time will tell if she's the right fit for this company.

STANDING on the sidewalk wrapped in the tattooed arms of a black-haired guy wearing glasses, Calliope Morrow gazes at the traffic as it whizzes by on the street in front of our apartment building.

I had my driver drop me off a block away after work so I could step into a floral boutique and pick up a bouquet.

I look down at it before I level my gaze at Champ.

She's wearing cut-off denim shorts and a black sweater.

She looks so damn sexy.

She left the office an hour before I did.

I know that because I saw her boarding the elevator with Delora by her side. Judging by the smiles on both of their faces, the day went well.

My day has gone to hell because now Champ is looking up and into the face of the tattooed guy.

Suddenly, her gaze shifts to the left and lands on me.

Fuck.

I toss her a wave. "Hey!"

She takes a step back from the guy who has been holding onto her for dear life.

It makes sense that she has a boyfriend. She's intelligent, spirited, and has an ass that I am struggling to keep my eyes off of.

The guy with her shoots me a look. "Who is that?"

The question is directed at Calliope, but I answer because I have plans, and my dinner date will give me shit if I'm late. "I'm her boss. I'm also her neighbor."

That sends the guy in my direction with his hand outstretched. "I'm Zeke."

I don't need or want to know that, but I'm not a complete

bastard, so I take his hand in mine for a brief shake. "Sean Wells."

"It's good to meet you," he says before tugging his hand away from mine. "I need to get going. I just stopped in for a quick visit."

"I'm glad you did," Calliope tells him. "Your surprise visits are one of my favorite things."

He turns back to face her. "Mine too."

I've heard enough, so I take a step toward the glass doors of the building. Lester, the doorman, rushes to open the door. That's going to cost me.

"Good evening, Mr. Wells," Lester says in a cheery tone. "How are you tonight, sir?"

I'm irritated as hell, but I don't put that on him.

Instead, I slide a bunch of bills from the pocket of my pants and shove them at him. "I'm fine, Lester."

Since he's blocking my path, I step to the left to get around him.

"This is very generous, sir," he whispers. "Very generous."

I acknowledge his gratitude with a smile and a pat on the shoulder.

"It was good to see you again, Mr. Morrow," Lester says as I walk into the lobby. "It's a joy having your sister living here."

What was that now?

I turn to see Calliope give the tattooed guy one last hug. "I'll call you later, Zeke."

"I'll answer." He chuckles. "Lock the apartment door once you're inside. Safety first, sis."

This guy is her brother.

Sensing that she's right behind me, I slow my pace as I walk toward the bank of elevators.

The soft scent of her perfume wafts through the air as she nears me.

"Those are beautiful flowers," she says as she steps in place beside me. "Your date will love those."

Jumping out onto a limb, I turn to look at her. "Our date."

Her eyebrows perk. "What?"

"We're having dinner with Mrs. Sweeney tonight, Champ." I motion for her to board the elevator when the doors slide open. "Get ready to have the best tuna casserole you've ever had."

Her nose scrunches. "Tuna casserole?"

"It's a hell of a lot better than it sounds."

CHAPTER ELEVEN

Callie

I'M unsure how I was roped into attending this dinner party, but I'm glad I'm here.

When Sean knocked on Mrs. Sweeney's door, she swung it open with a flourish.

She didn't seem the least bit surprised to find me standing next to him. She gathered me into her arms and welcomed me into her home without any hesitation.

Her apartment is a carbon copy of my brother's in terms of its layout, but that's where the similarities end.

The sofa and chair in her living room are a dusty blue color. The lamps have white shades with gold trim. There's a record player in the corner, and a silver tray with an elegant tea set on the coffee table.

As soon as I was inside, I felt as though I had been transported back in time to when I was nine. I spent two weeks with my grandma during the summer at her home in Vermont.

It had the same feel as this apartment. The same coziness engulfed me there.

"I've invited the Durkmans from the eleventh floor to join us tonight," Mrs. Sweeney says to Sean. "I know how much you enjoy their company."

He shoots me a look and mouths the words, "*I don't,*" before he smiles at her. "The more the merrier, right?"

"That's what I always say." She pats his forearm. "I'm going to mix us some drinks. Why don't you entertain Calliope while I do that?"

With one last lingering look at the bouquet of flowers in the vase in the middle of the dining room table, she starts toward the kitchen.

Sean turns to look at me. "Your brother seems nice."

I'm still surprised that he hasn't met Zeke before. "He is nice. My other brother, Grady, is nice too."

Dropping his gaze to my bare legs, he nods. "Maybe I'll meet him someday."

"You met him already."

He shakes his head. "I can't say that I have."

"He's your next-door neighbor," I point out.

"You're my next-door neighbor," he counters with a smile.

"I'm staying in Grady's apartment while he's working out of state," I explain. "He's lived in that apartment for almost a year. You must have met him at some point."

His chin lifts. "Tall guy? Brown hair? Looks nothing like you?"

All of that is true, so I nod. "That's him."

"I've seen him, but we've never met."

"Why not?"

He laughs. "He's never around. I don't know what your

brother does for a living, but I think I've passed him in the lobby twice."

That's not surprising at all. Grady's job sucks up all of his time. Before he left New York, I only saw him when he'd stop in the bar for a drink. That was a rare occurrence.

"He works too much," I mutter.

"Don't we all?" Sean chuckles. "I need to give you a heads-up. Mr. Durkman is an asshole. His wife is a sweetheart, though, so you focus on her. I'll handle her husband."

I plant both hands on my hips and step closer to where Sean is standing near the dining room table. "I have no trouble dealing with assholes."

"I know how you deal with assholes." He rubs his jaw. "You're not calling the police on old Durkman tonight, Champ. Don't ruin Mrs. Sweeney's party the way you ruined mine."

I hold in a smile. "Did you just admit that you're an asshole?"

A loud series of raps at Mrs. Sweeney's apartment door sends Sean in that direction. "Here we go. Consider this your initiation to the building, Calliope. You'll thank me later for keeping Durkman occupied."

"You seem sure of yourself."

He glances back at me. "I am."

I'VE HAD to bite my tongue at least ten times since Mrs. Sweeney served up tuna casserole with cheese biscuits on the side.

Surprisingly, it was a delicious meal.

At least, I thought it was.

Mr. Durkman was less complimentary.

He complained about the size of the tuna chunks, the type of noodles, the sauce it was swimming in, and the texture of the biscuits, among other things.

Each time he opened his mouth to insult Mrs. Sweeney's culinary skills, Sean put him in his place.

He didn't tell him to shut the hell up or to get out.

Instead, my boss pointed out that Mr. Durkman helped himself to seconds of everything. Then, Sean proceeded to shower Mrs. Durkman with compliments.

The gray-haired man wasn't fond of watching a much younger man flirt with his wife.

It was entertaining, but I'm ready to call it a night.

I'm still exhausted after spending half of last night pissed at my neighbor.

I glance in his direction to find him staring at me.

"I made chocolate pudding for dessert," Mrs. Sweeney announces as she pushes back from the table to stand. "I'll go get that."

"Is it homemade, or did you use an instant box mix?" Mr. Durkman questions.

All eyes shoot in his direction.

Unable to keep my opinion to myself a moment longer, I clear my throat. "Does it matter? Tonight isn't about the delicious meal, although it was incredibly kind of Mrs. Sweeney to prepare everything. Tonight is about community. We should all be grateful that we're here together."

I toned that down, but it conveys the message I want grumpy Mr. Durkman to receive.

"I'm damn grateful," Sean backs me up. "I'm so fucking grateful that I say we do this again next week. Same day. Same time, but I'll cook for everyone. What do you all say?"

Mrs. Sweeney and Mrs. Durkman agree immediately.

Mr. Durkman narrows his eyes behind his glasses. "What are you cooking?"

"Whatever it is, we all know you're going to eat it," Sean says. "You're responsible for dessert, so make it a good one."

A grin creeps over Mr. Durkman's lips for the first time tonight. "I'll agree to that."

Sean turns to look at me. "Are you in, Calliope? All you need to bring is that winning smile."

I gaze around the table. I don't know how I became a member of this dinner club, but it can't hurt to get to know my temporary neighbors better.

Although, the idea of getting to know Sean better is as exciting as it is terrifying.

"I'm in," I whisper. "I'll be there."

CHAPTER TWELVE

Sean

WHEN I CONJURED up the idea of giving my neighbor a ride to work every day, I forgot about the ass factor.

As in her perfect peach-shaped, lush ass.

Calliope is wearing a fitted pink dress today, and fuck me, that ass is making me feel all kinds of things.

It's mostly my cock feeling things as the bastard decided to harden as soon as I looked through the peephole in my apartment door and caught a glimpse of Champ's ass as she made her way to the elevator.

I should have sprinted after her to get on the lift too, but I needed to calm my dick down before I came face-to-face with my newest employee.

I'm in the midst of that now as I step in place next to where she's waiting on the sidewalk in front of our building.

"Good morning, Calliope," I say gruffly.

Her eyes snake up my dark blue suit and gray tie to my face. "Good morning, Mr. Wells."

Is that how it's going to be?

As much as I enjoy being called that, we're not just two people who work together. We're neighbors, and I don't want to draw a line in the sand on when she can or can't call me by my first name.

"Call me Sean," I tell her with a smile.

"All right," she says hesitantly. "Should I be calling your brother Mr. Wells?"

She should call him Decky because his head would explode, but my brother and I agreed to respect one another at the office, or at least attempt to.

"Declan is fine," I say as I glance over her head to the approaching traffic.

"Declan," she repeats softly. "Got it."

I take a step forward when I notice my black SUV approaching. The driver, Jurgen, raises a hand off the steering wheel in greeting. I offer him a nod in response.

Calliope glances at me. "This is your ride?"

"Our ride," I correct her. "The length of my work day varies, but Jurgen will be available to drive you home each day at six. I can't say for certain if I'll be along for that ride on any given day."

As Jurgen gets out and rounds the car, Calliope steps forward. "I appreciate that, but I won't always come straight home from work each day. Sometimes, like today, I have plans."

I watch her ass as she climbs into the back seat of the vehicle.

I shake off the thought of what it would be like to take her from behind and instead focus on what she just said as I follow her into the car. "You have plans?"

In no realm within the business world is it appropriate for me to ask that. It's the same reason why I haven't drilled her on whether or not she has a boyfriend.

I'm her boss, and there are limits to what I can inquire about.

Her gaze skims my face. "That's right. I have plans."

That tells me nothing.

I turn my attention to the window and watch the countless people rushing by on the sidewalk in pursuit of another day at work.

"I appreciate the ride to work, Sean," she says softly.

I look at her only to find her staring at me. "It's my pleasure, Champ."

That coaxes a soft smile to her lips. "I'm excited to prove to you what I'm capable of. I know I'll be a great asset to Wells."

I cock a brow. "You already landed the job. Save that enthusiasm for your first campaign. You're about to discover that I'm not easy to impress."

Her smile doesn't falter. In fact, it widens even more. "There's a lot more to me than meets the eye. I'm confident you'll be more than satisfied with what I bring to the table."

With that, she turns her attention to the window next to her as Jurgen steers the car into the morning traffic of Manhattan.

There is something so fucking irresistible about a confident woman. Add a drop-dead gorgeous face, a body made for sin, and an ability to spar effortlessly with me.

Calliope Morrow is a goddamn force of nature, and the fact that she may be going out with some undeserving fool tonight is the only thing I can think about.

"IT LOOKS like you're doing some actual work today." My brother's voice breaks through the fog of my thoughts as he wanders into my office through the open doorway.

"Back up and shut the damn door," I say in response. "Then knock so I can tell you to get lost."

Declan sits his ass in one of the chairs that face my desk. "We need to go over the new distribution deal."

We both know that we don't need to handle that alone.

We employ people who are highly skilled at negotiating contracts that will land our products in more stores worldwide.

The fact is that neither of us is willing to give up that level of control.

We began this as a two-person endeavor, and we're still committed to that regardless of how many lawyers or brilliant business minds we've hired.

My brother crosses his legs, skimming his palm over the thigh of his black trousers. "What's on your mind, Sean?"

"The distribution deal," I say.

He ignores that blatant lie and presses me. "What's really on your mind? You've been preoccupied all morning."

Calliope has been on my mind.

It got so bad that I did something I had no right to an hour ago.

I scoured her social media profiles for anything that would give me a clue about her life.

I came up empty. Everything is set to private. Her profile images are all the same stunning photo of the Brooklyn Bridge.

"Are you thinking about a woman?" Declan reaches a conclusion that I can't fault him for. "Is it someone from the party the other night? I saw you getting cozy with a redhead."

"The redhead with the bleeding nose?" I question him. "I was administering first aid."

"Sure you were." His arms cross his chest. "I appreciate that you threw me a birthday party. Next time try inviting a few people I know."

I laugh that off. "You knew at least ninety percent of the people there."

His left brow perks.

"You knew at least half of the people there," I amend my estimate. "I can't help if the people I invited spread that invitation around."

"Speaking of invites." He drops his gaze to the watch on his wrist. "I'm here to invite you to lunch. You name the place."

I chuckle. "I get to choose? Who are you, and what the fuck did you do with Decky?"

"Not funny," he says with a straight face. "It's a limited-time offer, so get a move on."

I round my desk en route to the door. Declan falls in step behind me to pat me in the center of the back. "I stopped in to check on Callie. She's fitting in just fine."

I glance at his face, trying to gauge whether his interest in her reaches beyond his position as her boss.

I come up empty.

"She's confident she'll have something substantial to offer for our next campaign," I paraphrase what Calliope said to me.

"Good." He shoves both hands in the front pocket of his pants. "We need to move in a new direction. That billboard in Times Square has to go."

I laugh in response. "I'm the CEO, remember? I get last say on that."

"I know." He shakes his head. "That's how we ended up

here in the first place. Name another CEO who appears in their print campaign."

I start rattling off the names of a couple of tech bigwigs and the well-known owner of a mobile phone company.

Declan stops me with a raise of a finger in the air. "All of them had a shirt and pants on in their campaigns."

I smooth a hand over my chest and stomach. "None of them had all of this to work with."

He barks out a laugh. "I'm putting a hell of a lot of faith in Callie. I need you and your dick off that billboard as soon as possible."

CHAPTER THIRTEEN

Callie

"I'M SORRY." I lean closer to where Delora is sitting. "Can you repeat that?"

"I said that Mr. Wells is the star of our current campaign."

I swear my brain is short-circuiting right now because I'm tempted to ask her to repeat that yet again.

"Not Mr. D," she whispers. "It's Mr. S. That's Sean on the billboard in Times Square."

I stare blankly at her in response.

"I shouldn't admit this," she lowers her voice yet again. "If I were twenty years younger, I'd make a move on him."

I shake my head. "Are you telling me that Mr. Wells is the model?"

"Bingo!" She nods. "It's unorthodox, but when we were searching for a model for the campaign, Sean kept telling me that my choices were shit."

I cringe.

She bats a hand over mine. "It's typical Sean. When he

announced he would be the model, I admit I wasn't on board until his shirt came off."

She fans a hand in front of her face.

I glance at the open door to the conference room we're sitting in. It was her idea to sneak in here for our first official meeting. I was grateful because the cubicle she assigned me is sandwiched between two others.

My new co-workers seem great, but they've already built a rapport with one another and, so far, I've felt like a third wheel. It's only my second day on the job, so I know I'll find my place in time.

"Declan wants us to come up with something new and fresh for the winter campaign." She rolls her eyes. "I've been doing this a very long time, and there are only so many ways you can push a pair of underwear at the world."

I smile. "I can jot down a few ideas if that would be helpful."

It's a tentative way of injecting myself into the middle of planning the upcoming campaign. Delora mentioned the campaign briefly during my interview, but it hasn't come up since.

I know I'm the newest member of the marketing team, but I feel I have a lot to offer, so I'll remind my boss of that every chance I get.

"That would be very helpful." She drops her gaze to her phone's screen. "We'll have a brainstorming session next week. Everyone is welcome to toss out any ideas that pop into their heads."

Excitement nips at me.

I plan on starting on a list of ideas right away.

"I want you to take a look at our social media accounts this week, " she says. "I know there is room for improvement there."

"I'll get started on that today."

"Are you free for dinner tonight?" she asks with a smile.

I'm going to hop on the subway headed to Queens after work to have dinner with my sister and her kids. Harlan is working late, so I volunteered to drop by to help prepare dinner and read bedtime stories.

"I'm only asking because when I mentioned to Sean that I wanted to take you out for a welcome aboard dinner, he mumbled that he thinks you have a date." She laughs. "I don't know how he would know that. He's not a mind reader."

I didn't realize Sean was paying that much attention this morning when I told him I had plans after work. It's amusing that he assumed those plans involve a date.

I glance at Delora. Something tells me that if I give her a detailed accounting of where I'm going after work, she'll report that back to Sean.

My personal life is none of his business, so I nod. "I do have plans tonight. I'm free tomorrow night if you are."

Her face brightens with a wide smile. "I'm free as a bird. I'll make a reservation for tomorrow night after work."

"Works for me," I say.

She pushes back from the table. "I think you're going to be a perfect fit for Wells, Callie."

I take that as a good sign.

"I'll get to work on looking over the social media accounts." I move to stand too. "Thank you for giving me this chance, Delora."

She starts toward the conference room door. "There was something about your interview that stuck with me. Before you walked out the door, I knew that you would be my pick."

I take pride in that.

I couldn't have anticipated that I'd be living next door to my boss, but that's temporary. There's a chance I can build a long-lasting career here at Wells. I want that, so I need to stay committed to doing the very best job I can.

"SHUT THE FRONT DOOR." Naomi's eyes widen. "You're telling me that the hottie that lives next door to Grady is the underwear model?"

I knew having a glass of wine was a bad idea.

When I got to my sister's house, she was pulling vegetables out of the fridge that she said she needed to use up. She decided to throw it all on a sheet pan and roast it. The crusty bread I picked up on my way over here was a perfect accompaniment to that.

The last item she yanked out of the fridge was an almost empty bottle of red wine.

I offered to finish it off.

Wine always makes me relax. Today I may have had one sip too many because when my sister asked if I'd met the Times Square billboard model, I blurted out that he's not only my boss but my neighbor too.

"I live next door to him now," I remind her. "Technically, he's my temporary neighbor."

She glances to where her kids are playing with a stack of wooden blocks. "Technically, he's fuckable as fuck."

Grateful that she's lowering her voice so her kids can't hear, I shake my head. "He's my boss, Naomi."

"He's also a hot as hell man." She giggles. "Why not mix business with pleasure? What do you have to lose?"

"The best job I've ever had." I push the wine glass away from me. "Besides, he's not my type at all. He's loud and obnoxious. He's an egomaniac. He put himself on a billboard. Who does that?"

"A smart businessman with the body of a model," she says with a straight face. "I think it's a brilliant move on his part."

I slide the glass closer again but don't pick it up. "How so?"

"Why hire someone to wear your product if you look that good?" She steals a glance at her kids. "He made the right choice, Callie. That billboard gets a hell of a lot of attention."

Not convinced by her argument, I shake my head. "He's full of himself. I've sworn off men like that."

Pushing up from the table, she sighs. "Don't let your past dictate your future. Not all rich men are like Dagen."

I don't want to talk about my ex, so I change the subject. "I'm on cleanup duty. Why don't you play with the kids?"

"Thank you." She squeezes my shoulder. "There is nothing wrong with a little after work fun with the boss. Don't knock it until you've tried it."

I groan and laugh at the same time. "I'm not trying it. I won't be sleeping with my boss."

"Keep your options open." She smiles. "Sometimes, a man like that can surprise a woman like you."

That might be true, but I'm still dealing with the fallout from my breakup six months ago. The last thing I need is to get entangled with someone like Sean Wells.

CHAPTER FOURTEEN

Sean

A QUICK STOP at Tin Anchor earlier this evening didn't reap the reward I wanted. I hoped that I'd get a chance to indulge in a glass of scotch while staring at my newest employee.

Apparently, the *plans* she spoke of had nothing to do with her second job.

Delora mentioned that she'd asked Champ to join her for dinner, but she got the same song and dance about Calliope's plans.

Since I'm trying to nail down the respectful boss thing, I dropped the idea of tracking her down.

It wouldn't have been hard.

One phone call and a bullshit marketing emergency, and I would have blown those plans apart. The problem is that our current marketing campaign is running smoothly.

I sprint up the concrete steps leading up to a brownstone on the Upper East Side.

I bang my fist against the door in a series of knocks that make no sense to anyone but the person who lives here and me.

It doesn't take much more than a few seconds before the next sequence of knocks in our secret code sound from the opposite side of the door.

As the door swings open, I bark out a laugh.

My gaze lands on the muscular chest of one of my best friends.

"What the fuck, Harry?" I question him. "Put on a goddamn shirt."

His hand runs the length of his chest and abs before it settles on his hip, just above the waistband of his black sweatpants. "Says the guy who is practically naked in Times Square."

Harrison Keene, along with my other two closest friends, Graham Locke and Kavan Bane, are the only people outside those employed by Wells who know I'm the guy in that print ad.

I brush past him on my way inside his home.

It's all old-world charm mixed with modern design.

Harry bought the place from his uncle years ago. For a time, it was my home too. Harry was going through a rough patch, and I wanted to lend a hand.

That had nothing to do with monetary aid.

I wanted to be around in case he needed a friend or someone to whip up dinner.

Harry, Kavan, and Graham are as close to me as Declan is.

Harry trails behind me as I make my way through the foyer, into the main hallway, and straight to the kitchen.

When I round the island in pursuit of a cold beer from the

fridge, I finally glance back to catch him yanking a T-shirt over his head. It's emblazoned with the logo of the boarding school we attended when we were teenagers. It makes sense given that Harry foot the bill for The Buchanan School's new library, which opened two months ago.

His brown hair is mussed, and he's covered in sweat from what must have been a hard workout in his home gym.

"How are you feeling?" I ask the question that always slips out even though it irks Harry whenever it leaves my lips.

"I'm good," he says as he rakes a hand through his hair, trying to smooth it back into place. "What are you doing here?"

I bend down to look in the fridge. Just as I suspect, it's fully stocked with organic fruits and vegetables and free-range chicken and beef.

"I'm here to cook you dinner."

I glance to where he's standing. He's grinning from ear to ear. "I won't turn that down, but why are you really here, Sean?"

I yank two bottles of imported beer from the fridge and place them on the island before sliding open the drawer that holds the bottle opener. "No reason other than I missed your pretty face."

His blue eyes narrow as he considers my words. "If I get one of your home-cooked meals out of this, I suppose the reason doesn't matter."

"It doesn't," I agree.

"I'm going to hit the shower." He glances at the now opened bottles of beer. "I'll be back in twenty. I'm in the mood for steak if you're curious."

Expecting to hear that, I chuckle. "Steak it is, Harry."

I didn't plan on showing up on his doorstep, but it beats

sitting in my apartment waiting for a glimpse of Calliope through the peephole when she gets home from her date.

As hard as I try, I can't stop thinking about what it would be like to have her naked beneath me.

CHAPTER FIFTEEN

Callie

IT TOOK me two blocks before I realized why my niece and nephew were giggling when I hugged them goodbye.

By then, I was on the platform of a subway stop in Queens.

There, a woman walked up next to me, leaned in close, and told me that I had two small blue handprints on my ass.

Those handprints belong to Tabitha.

It was my brilliant idea to bust out the finger painting set I had bought Bodhi for his birthday.

Tabitha dove into the blue paint with enthusiasm. Bodhi was much more restrained as he dipped each of his fingertips in a different color before he painted what looked like an absolute masterpiece on a sheet of paper.

My niece took her talent to the wall in the kitchen, then the refrigerator, and finally my dress.

I knew she touched me, but I was too busy scrubbing the paint from the wall to put two and two together.

I hold my head high as I walk into the lobby of my building. I've made it this far with the two tiny handprints on the skirt of my pink dress. Surely, I can manage to get from here to my apartment without anyone saying another word about it.

I breeze past the doorman with a wave of my hand in his direction.

I'm grateful it's not Lester because he always rushes toward me when I arrive home. I don't know if he's in search of a tip or just a friendly hello. I haven't put more than a few dollars in his palm since moving in. I can't afford it right now, and besides, Grady told me that he overtips the doormen, so I shouldn't worry about it.

I approach the bank of elevators with quick steps. Just as I jab my finger into the call button, I hear heavy footsteps behind me.

"Please don't let it be him," I whisper. "Please."

The last thing I need is my boss to catch me like this.

The footsteps slow, and I know the person is right behind me. It's a man. I can tell from the scent of cologne that is filling the air. It smells divine.

I take another whiff and silently curse because it's the same cologne I smelled on my way to work this morning.

"Champ." His deep voice cuts into me.

Why does he have the sexiest voice I've ever heard?

I don't turn to glance at him. "Saint."

"From where I'm standing, it looks like you had one hell of a night."

Holding back a smile, I shake my head. Maybe if I play dumb, he'll let it go. "I have no idea what you're talking about."

The elevator dings, and before he can say anything in response, the doors slide open.

I step in and wait to turn around until I know he's next to me.

I keep my gaze on the panel on the wall as I press the button for our floor.

"It looks like your date had tiny hands." He leans closer, so his arm is brushing against my shoulder. "You know what they say about men with tiny hands."

To punctuate that point, he holds up his hands in front of him, his large hands.

I shake my head. "I know what they say about men who assume things."

"I'm pretty sure you're calling me an ass," he says. "Maybe I have it all wrong, and there's another explanation for those blue handprints on your dress. Did that guy in the Smurf costume in Times Square get handsy with you?"

I finally turn my gaze so I can look up into his face. "What if he did?"

"I'll kick his fucking ass."

I can't help but smile. "Keep your fists to yourself. My niece decided to use anything she could find as her canvas tonight when she was finger painting."

He leans back and glances down as if he's trying to steal another look at the back of my dress. "You should save the dress as is. The kid may have a future in art, and you could be wearing a goldmine."

I step forward as the elevator lurches to a stop on our floor. "I think I'll tempt fate and let the dry cleaner work their magic."

As the doors slide open, he motions for me to exit first. "If that's the plan, I need to get one last look at the work of art before it disappears forever."

I stay in place. "In that case, why don't you go first?"

Laughing, he steps forward. "Good night, Calliope. I'll see you in the morning."

I press my finger on the button to hold the doors open until he disappears behind his apartment door. Once he's out of sight, I draw a sigh of relief. All I want to do tonight is sit in a bubble bath and think about anything but my neighbor.

CHAPTER SIXTEEN

Sean

TEASING Calliope on the way up to our floor put a smile on my face and made me hard.

By the time I walked into my apartment twenty minutes ago, I was aching to come.

I did that in the shower as I envisioned what she looks like beneath the paint-stained dress.

Does she wear lace or silk panties? What color are her nipples? Is her mound smooth or trimmed?

I jacked off thinking about all of those details and more.

Chasing those thoughts away with a shake of my head, I tug on a pair of pajama bottoms. Striding across my bedroom floor on bare feet, I move toward where I dropped my phone on my bed.

I scoop it into my palm and scan the screen, glancing at all the notifications that have arrived in the past ten minutes.

Owning a business is both a blessing and a curse.

The curse is never-ending small details that have to be

taken care of. Every problem that surfaces falls in either Declan's lap or mine.

Tonight it looks like the bulk of it is directed to me.

I shoot back a few responses to text messages sent by employees looking for direction in the areas of shipping or quality control.

We're a twenty four hour, seven day a week operation. The sun never goes down on Wells.

I continue scanning my unread texts looking for anything else that requires my immediate attention.

A soft knock on my apartment door sends my gaze toward the hallway.

I toss the phone on my bed and head out in that direction.

Shirtless.

My body is on display in the epicenter of the world. Whoever needs my attention right now has likely already seen it.

I swing open the door to find a stranger.

She's petite, blonde, and attractive, but I'm at a loss as to who the hell she is.

My arms cross my chest as her gaze slides over me slowly.

"Well, hello, handsome." Her voice trails as her fingers move to touch my arm.

I step back so I'm just out of her reach. "Can I help you?"

Her blue-eyed gaze wanders behind me. "I know you can. I think I lost an earring in your bed. I need it back."

A soft sound behind her pulls my eyes in that direction.

Calliope, dressed in those sexy-as-fuck denim cut-off shorts and a pink T-shirt, is standing at her door.

"Ignore me." She lets out an awkward laugh. "I'm just getting back from the dry cleaner."

A finger tapping my chest lures my gaze back to the blonde in front of me. I reach forward to grab her hand so she will stop fucking touching me. "Your earring isn't in my bed."

I catch one last glimpse of Calliope before she disappears behind her apartment door.

"I was here the other night," the blonde explains. "I had to lay down for a minute, so I was in your bed. My earring must have fallen off."

Fucking hell.

Since the door to my bedroom was locked because I don't want random people screwing in my bed, she has to be talking about the guest room.

It hasn't been cleaned since then, so I step aside to let her in.

I point at a spot on the floor just inside the entryway. "Stay right here. I'll go look for it."

"It's a gold hoop," she calls after me. "I wouldn't mind coming to look with you."

The trailing giggle that follows is an invitation to fuck her.

A month ago, I would have RSVPed by hauling her over my shoulder and keeping her for the night, but that was before I knew Champ existed.

Scowling, I drop to my ass on the guest bed and start the hunt for the earring.

I snatch it up just as I hear a noise behind me.

I turn to see the pretty blonde with wide eyes and a broad smile on her mouth.

"I couldn't wait by the door. I'm not patient," she explains as her hand toys with the strap of the tank top she's wearing. "I'm not looking for anything serious if you're in the mood for some fun."

I slide off the bed, walk toward her and drop the earring in her palm. "I'm in the mood for sleep, so I'll see you out."

She's silent until we reach the door to my apartment. "Has anyone ever told you that your chest and abs look a lot like that beast on the billboard in Times Square?"

I swing open my apartment door. "No, but thanks?"

She chuckles. "Thanks, indeed. I enjoyed whatever this was, and my offer still stands in case you change your mind."

She has a business card out of her purse before I can get a word in.

She shoves it at me, turns on her heel, and marches out the door.

Without a glance at it, I crush the card into a ball and toss it in the wastebasket in my foyer.

Then, I lock my door and head to my bedroom to watch a movie before calling it a night.

CHAPTER SEVENTEEN

CALLIE

AS I EXIT my building to wait for Jurgen, I glance down at my hands.

When I finally got out of the bathtub last night, my fingers were as wrinkled as prunes.

I must have soaked in the warm water for almost an hour because, by the time I got out, all of the bubbles were gone, and the water was chilled.

I crawled into it right after I got back from the dry cleaner.

As soon as I took off my paint-stained dress, I knew it needed emergency intervention. Thankfully, the dry cleaner assured me it would be a breeze to clean.

Since it's one of my favorite dresses, I was on cloud nine until I was on my way back up to my apartment. I took that elevator trip with a woman who was headed for Sean's door.

I should have known that based on the fact that she

applied an extra layer of lipstick during our journey, and spritzed some heavenly-smelling perfume on the base of her neck.

As she exited the elevator, I lingered in the hallway and got way more than I bargained for.

I saw Sean Wells half-naked.

Even though I've seen him on the billboard, getting a full-on glimpse of him without a shirt on was mind-blowing.

"Are you thinking about me, Champ?"

The sound of his voice sends my gaze to the right at breakneck speed. I swear I almost gave myself whiplash.

I glimpse at his handsome face. "No. Why?"

He tilts his chin back a touch. "You're blushing."

Dammit.

It's a curse. Every time I get the slightest bit aroused, my cheeks flush. He can never know that, so I deflect. "It's warm out this morning. The weather is sure nice lately, isn't it?"

He cocks a dark eyebrow. "Weather is weather."

Of course he's not the type of man you can engage in small talk with.

He gazes jumps from the red dress I'm wearing to the approaching traffic. "What's on the agenda for today?"

"Work." I smile. "I'll come up with a few brilliant ideas, and then I'm having dinner with my boss."

His eyes search my face. "Is that your way of asking me out?"

I feel my cheeks flush more, so I turn to watch the people walking toward us. "I'm having dinner with Delora."

"The infamous Delora welcome dinner." He laughs. "She's going to take you to a French restaurant. She'll tell you that she rarely has red wine but will pound back two bottles in record time. Be prepared to hear about her three ex-husbands. The second one was the love of her life, but he dumped her for her sister. The first is her current boyfriend. Don't be surprised if she's sexting him throughout dinner."

I shake my head. "What?"

Jurgen honks the horn as he approaches where we're standing. "You're welcome, Champ."

I take a step toward the car as it slows to a stop. "I didn't say thank you."

Sean opens the back passenger door before Jurgen is out of the car. "You will when I conveniently show up just in time for dessert tonight."

I can't tell if he's joking, so I silently get into the car while trying to absorb everything he just told me.

―――

ACROSS THE TABLE FROM ME, Delora giggles as she types something into her phone.

We're at Sérénité, a French restaurant on Tenth Avenue. When we arrived, I had to bite back a smile because Sean nailed that detail this morning when he was describing how my evening would play out.

That smile faded quickly as Delora ordered an expensive bottle of red wine. Before I was done half of my first glass, she had polished off the entire bottle and was onto the second.

I've heard details I never should have known about all three of Delora's marriages.

If Sean's last prediction is accurate, she's currently in the midst of a sexting spree with her first ex-husband. His name escapes me because everything became a blur after she told me about her wedding night with her second husband.

That's a conversation that should be filed away for eternity under '*never should have happened.*'

I take a sip of wine while Delora feverishly taps her fingers against her phone's screen, stopping briefly to take a side-eyed selfie complete with duck lips.

How the hell did Sean know all of this would happen?

As if on cue, I glance up toward the entrance of the restaurant to see my savior on the approach.

Is this where the Saint nickname stems from?

Does he swoop in and save people from horrendously uncomfortable situations?

Sean shoots me a smile as he nears our table. He sends another one in the direction of our waiter. He's a friendly, patient guy who seems to be in his early twenties.

The waiter nods as if Sean sent him a silent message.

I watch as Sean grabs a vacant chair from a nearby table. He keeps his gaze trained on mine as he steps up next to Delora.

"What do we have here?"

His voice startles Delora enough that her phone juggles in her hands before it falls to her lap.

"Sean," she says his name in a breathless rush. "What are you doing here?"

He sets the chair down and drops onto it, so he's sitting between the two of us. "How's the wine, Delora?"

"So good," she murmurs. "I'm just finishing up something with Larry. I'll be back in two minutes."

Sean doesn't say anything until she's nearing the ladies' restroom. "She'll be gone for at least the next fifteen. Dean is bringing you a big brownie sundae, Champ."

"Dean?" I question.

"Your waiter," he says, his gaze dropping to the red dress

I've been wearing all day. "You need that dessert after what you've been through tonight."

I grin. "Thank you."

A slow smile spreads across his lips. "It's my pleasure, Calliope."

CHAPTER EIGHTEEN

S̲ean

I TRAIL Calliope as we leave the restaurant.

Our time spent with Delora after she '*finished with Larry*' was fun.

She told a couple of good-natured stories about the early days of Wells. Back then, Declan and I were flying by the seat of our collective pants. We were drawing on words of wisdom bestowed upon us by our grandfather, Stetson Wells. Stetson founded one of the most successful whiskey brands in the country when he was old enough to consume it legally.

He built it up with hard work and determination until he sold it shortly before his death. I hated him for that. It was always my dream to take that company's reins one day. At my grandfather's funeral I found out that my older brother carted that same dream around with him.

Declan went to law school to appease our mother, but his career path changed after graduating.

With part of our joint inheritances from the old man, we launched Wells.

It's taken grit and a hell of a lot of stubborn resolve, but we've accomplished not only our wildest dreams, we've also surpassed them ten times over.

Once we're clear of the crowds exiting Sérénité, Calliope glances over her shoulder at me. "Have you met Larry?"

"Yeah," I mumble. "Unfortunately, I have."

That turns her around to face me. "Unfortunately? What does that mean?"

I shove both hands in the front pockets of my pants. "Larry is a hugger."

Her index finger jumps to the side of her nose. She scratches it lightly, drawing my gaze to that exact spot. "You don't like hugging?"

"I fucking love it," I say, still transfixed with her nose. "You have a tiny diamond stud in your nose."

Her fingertip taps it before she drops her hand. "I got it back in high school. I kind of like it."

I kind of do, too, along with the rest of her breathtaking face, her laugh, the scent of her perfume, and her ability to pack away an entire dessert while still looking elegant and graceful.

"What's Larry like?" she questions.

"Why?" I study her face wondering if I've missed anything else. "He's off the market. It's only a matter of time before he pops the question to Delora again."

Her blue eyes widen under heavy lashes. "You think she's going to get married for the fourth time?"

"I know she will," I say with confidence. "If Delora likes one thing more than a good bottle of wine, it's a husband."

A scowl mars her perfect face. "I can't fathom that."

I glance past her to where people are walking on the sidewalk. "Larry's a good guy. Granted, he grabbed my ass when he hugged me, but he said he was checking out the quality of my pants, so I let it slide."

Calliope laughs. "You're not serious?"

"Dead serious." My arms cross my chest. "Overall, he's a decent guy. He loves Delora, and I think she loves him too in her own way."

"But they already divorced once." Confusion knits her brow and taints her words. "Why put yourself back in the middle of a relationship that has already failed?"

I sense there's a hell of a lot more to the question, so I ask one. "Have you ever been married, Calliope?"

Her eyes bore into mine. "Have you?"

Deflection is a clever tool unless the person you're attempting to use it on is more of a master at it than you are.

I step closer to her. "I haven't taken that plunge. Have you?"

There's no way in hell I'm dropping this. Curiosity has a death grip on me, and it's not going to let go until I know something, anything, about this woman's personal life.

"I was engaged," she admits. "Once."

"When?" That shoots out from between my lips before I can think it through.

She studies me as if she's weighing the consequences of answering. "It ended about six months ago."

Her gaze trails away from my face to the steady flow of traffic in front of the restaurant.

I summoned Jurgen five minutes ago, so he'll be rounding the corner at any moment. We'll get into the car. She'll share small talk with my driver until we're home and the night will end.

I'm not ready for that.

"Let's get a drink," I suggest.

"A drink?" she echoes.

"One drink," I clarify. "I can give you the inside scoop on Delora, so you have a leg up when dealing with her. For instance, if you bring her a dozen freshly baked chocolate chip cookies on a Friday morning, she'll give you the afternoon off."

A smile plays on her lips. "Isn't that bribery?"

"Damn right it is, but it works like a fucking charm."

Her hand dives into her purse to retrieve her phone. She types something on the screen. "I'm making a note of that. It could come in handy."

"I've got a hundred more tips like that." I glance to the left as Jurgen steers the car next to the curb. "Are you in the mood for a drink?"

Her gaze volleys between the car and my face. "One drink won't hurt."

Famous last words.

CHAPTER NINETEEN

CALLIE

I DO a quick scan of the bar we just entered.

That's a habit born from working part-time at my favorite bar in this city.

I didn't catch the name of this place when Jurgen pulled the car up to the curb in front of it, but it's even more of a hole-in-the-wall type establishment than Tin Anchor is.

Peanuts overflow from a bowl set atop the wooden bar. An older man wearing glasses is behind it, with a bar towel in his hand.

He gazes in our direction as Sean motions for me to take a spot on a wooden stool next to the bar. I shimmy onto it, being mindful of the front slit in the skirt of my dress.

Sean follows my movements with his gaze while taking a seat next to me.

"Sean!" The bartender approaches us. "I haven't seen you in weeks. How are you?"

"Good," Sean responds. "I'm good, Rolly."

Rolly tips his chin up to peer down his nose at me. "Who do we have here?"

"This is Champ," Sean makes the introduction. "I'll have whatever she's having."

That sends my gaze in his direction. I quiz him silently with a lift of my left eyebrow.

"I trust you." He chuckles. "Make me proud."

I tug on my right earring as I consider the possibilities. I'm reasonably sure that he'd order a glass of scotch if he came in here alone, but there's something to be said for expanding your alcoholic repertoire.

"We'll have two Tom Collins," I tell the bartender.

"Coming right up," Rolly says before he steps away from us.

Sean glances in my direction. "I can't say I've ever tasted a Tom before."

My eyes meet his. "I have."

He's quick to respond. "Don't tell me your ex was named Tom. That's one part of the relationship I don't want to hear about."

That suggests that there are parts of the relationship he does want to hear about. I have no interest in discussing my ex with him.

I pluck the scattered peanuts off the bar and pile them onto a small napkin in front of me. "You lured me here with the promise of insider information on my boss."

His gaze travels over my face. "That I did."

Pushing the napkin and peanuts to the side, I smile. "Give it to me. I promise I won't use that information for any nefarious purposes."

"You shouldn't make promises like that before you know the level of dirt I'm about to dish out."

I laugh softly. "Something tells me that you won't be selling Delora out tonight. There is no dirt, is there?"

He holds both hands up as though he's surrendering to me. "No dirt, but I can tell you how to handle her in a way that will make you her star employee."

We're interrupted when Rolly arrives with our drinks. I thank him with an added smile because I know how it feels when a person doesn't acknowledge the crafter of their beverage.

He thanks me for thanking him before he wanders off toward a man who just sat down at the opposite end of the bar.

Sean picks up the glass in front of him and takes a small sip. His eyes close. I can't tell if that's from disgust or delight.

"Not bad," he murmurs. "This isn't half bad."

I clear my throat. "Maybe I don't want to know how to handle Delora. Maybe I want to prove myself based solely on my merit."

Sean swallows his second taste of his Tom Collins. "Maybe I'm impressed by that."

Pride blooms inside of me from that admission, although I don't know why. Is it because he's my boss, or because he's not only gorgeous, he's fun and successful?

"Are you a scotch convert?" I ask as he raises the glass to his mouth again.

It stalls there, pressed against his bottom lip.

I tear my gaze away because staring at his mouth isn't what I should be doing.

"Too soon to tell." He laughs. "We'll need to meet again to continue this experiment."

Is he asking me out on a date?

I play dumb, hoping to lure more details of his intentions from him. "What experiment?"

His index finger rims his glass. "I like this, but I have a feeling that you make it better. If you're still holding onto that job at Tin Anchor, let me know when your next shift is, and I'll drop by to taste your Tom."

A smile plays on my lips. "I'll do that, Saint."

CHAPTER TWENTY

Sean

I PICK up a little pink dress and wave it in the air. "What about this?"

Graham Locke, my friend, and a soon-to-be girl dad, smiles. "I already bought that one for her."

This is the tenth time he's shot down my proposed gift for his baby girl in the past twenty minutes.

I approach where he's standing next to a display of children's books.

We're in a baby boutique on the Upper East Side. Who the hell knew a place like this even existed with its tiny cutesy clothes and gadgets for hiding stacks of diapers?

I feel like I stepped onto another planet when we walked in here after having lunch a block over.

"What haven't you bought?" I question him.

He rakes a hand through his dark brown hair. "Let me think."

I toss out my original idea for a baby gift. "I'm going to get that custom onesie made that I was telling you about."

Onesie.

That was another foreign concept to me until Graham announced that he was going to be a dad.

He did that during one of our Buck Boys dinners.

It's a term meant to pay homage to our time spent at The Buchanan School. Graham tells me he fucking hates being referred to as a Buck Boy, but secretly I think he loves it. I don't think Kavan or Harrison mind it either.

"No." His answer is direct. "My daughter is not wearing a onesie with your face on it."

I skim a hand over my neatly trimmed beard. "She'd love it, Locke."

"It would fucking terrify her."

I laugh that off as the shop owner approaches us.

She's a gray-haired woman with a penchant for pink.

Her outfit is light pink, her shoes a shade darker, and the ring on her finger is a sparkling pink diamond.

"Hi, Mr. Locke." She bats her eyelashes. "Back for more?"

Graham turns to her. "My friend is looking for a gift for Sela."

Little Sela Locke is due to arrive soon, and even though Graham thinks I've got nothing lined up in the gift department, I've already secured his baby girl's college education with a fund I set up a month ago.

This foray into baby-world-retail-land is so I can grab a few extra minutes with one of my best pals.

"A book is always a special something." The woman motions to the display. "I can help you pick out one, handsome."

I perk a brow. "I'll take one of each."

"Sean," Graham scolds me with a sharp bite of my name. "You don't need to do that."

I put a hand on his shoulder and squeeze it. "It's the least I can do. I plan on reading our girl a few bedtime stories. I need to be prepared for that."

The unexpected image of my grandmother sitting on the edge of my bed with a book in her hands when I was a kid shoots through my mind.

I remember those moments with fondness, and if I can create memories like that with Sela, I'm in.

"Thank you," Graham says in a genuine tone. "You're welcome to drop by whenever you want to read Sela a bedtime story."

That tugs at my heartstrings more than I'll admit, so I laugh it off as I face the boutique's owner again and hand her my credit card. "Pack them up to be delivered to Graham's home. I have a meeting I need to get to."

SITTING in on my brother's mid-afternoon meeting was a lesson in diplomacy. He can skillfully handle anyone with charm and grace.

On the other hand, I would have fired the entire accounting department for their recent missteps.

Declan chastised them in a way that will make them want to do better for him.

I know because I've been on the receiving end of my older brother's disappointment a time or two, and it's always pushed me to want to be a better person.

"Your thoughts, Saint?" Declan poses that question to me as I follow him into his office from the conference room.

"You're a better man than I'll ever be."

He laughs that off. "Everyone deserves a second chance, Sean."

I shut the door behind me. "I get that part of the accounting fuck ups had to do with software errors but you have to admit, that at least one of them should have caught the issue sooner."

He shrugs that off. "It was caught."

"After three days." I wave three fingers in the air.

He mimics my movements but with four of his fingers. "It's better than four days."

I can't argue that point, so I don't. "What are you doing tonight?"

That draws his gaze to my face. "Why?"

It's been years since I've arranged a blind double date for us, but his mind always wanders back to the night we had our last one. It was a shit show. The women we met up with were thirty years our senior.

They spent the bulk of dinner schooling us in good manners even though we were as polite as possible.

"I'm cooking dinner for a few people in my building," I tell him. "You're welcome to join us."

He shrugs that off with a shake of his head. "I'm hitting the gym."

"That's going to take all night?"

He flexes his bicep under the sleeve of his suit jacket. "If you wanted to look like this, you'd know it takes commitment, Saint."

"Go to hell." I laugh as I turn to exit his office.

"Only if you lead the way," he calls after me as I shut the door on my way out.

CHAPTER TWENTY-ONE

CALLIE

MY MOM TAUGHT me to never show up to dinner at someone's house without a gift in hand.

That's why I'm carrying a potted cactus.

I had no idea what to bring to Sean's apartment for dinner.

The man is rich, so it's not as though he needs anything. I know that he pinned dessert duties on Mr. Durkman, so something as innocuous as a plant seemed fitting.

Sean doesn't strike me as the type of person who has a green thumb, so I suspect the cactus will thrive in his presence. I've caught sight of a two-person cleaning crew exiting my neighbor's apartment early every second Saturday, so I'm hopeful they'll mind the cactus when they're there.

I take one last look at my outfit. I opted for a yellow sundress and low-heeled sandals. I wanted to look casual yet respectful, given that most of the dinner guests were born more than eighty years ago.

I knock on Sean's door.

I'm five minutes late. I felt that was acceptable since I didn't want to be the first to arrive.

The door swing opens, bringing with it the scent of something mouth-watering, along with the image of something just as appetizing.

Sean has lost the suit jacket he was wearing earlier. The sleeves of his light blue dress shirt are pushed up to his elbows, and his tie is nowhere in sight.

The two undone buttons at the top of his shirt show the smooth skin that hides beneath the fabric.

"Champ," he greets me with the nickname I'm growing fond of. "Welcome."

I smile. "Thank you. I brought you something."

His gaze drops to my hands and the gray clay pot that contains the small cactus. "How did you know?"

"Know what?" I ask as I shove it at him.

He takes it in his hands. "That I love these things."

"Cactuses?" The word comes out muffled in a slight chuckle.

He steps aside and motions for me to enter his apartment.

The last time I was at his door, I caught a glimpse of the expansive space over his shoulder, but this is incredible.

The living area alone has to be twice the size of Grady's entire apartment. The view of the city beyond the wall of windows is spectacular, as are the furnishings. I would have expected dark, intense tones from a man like him, but everything is crisp, white, and polished.

The warmth of vibrant potted plants everywhere sets it all off perfectly.

I lose count when I reach twelve. He must have at least double that just in this room alone.

"You have a green thumb?"

The question sends his gaze to mine. "Damn right I do. I'll add your contribution to that table by the window."

He sets off in his dress shoes, tapping a soft beat of his footsteps against the floor.

I glance to the left and then the right expecting to see the rest of his dinner party guests, but I come up empty.

When I look back at Sean, he's smiling at me. "The rest of our crew is on the way. When you've lived as long as they have, you shouldn't be in a rush to get anywhere."

Nerves spark somewhere inside of me. I try to brush the feeling away by silently convincing myself that this is just a dinner party between neighbors. This isn't the start of a date.

Sean walks toward me with his hands sunk in the front pockets of his pants. "In my excitement over the cactus, did I neglect to mention how goddamn beautiful you look tonight?"

"Thank you," I whisper. "You smell great."

Both of his brows pop. "Thanks, Champ. It's the new Matiz cologne. It costs a fucking fortune, but it was worth every penny if you're into it."

A squeak of a giggle bubbles out of me. "I meant that the dinner smells great."

He nods. "Sure you did. It's a rack of lamb, risotto, and grilled asparagus. Durkman is bringing dessert. Don't expect much. I'm betting on rice cereal treats."

"I like rice cereal treats," I admit.

He taps his forehead with the tip of his index finger. "I'm making a mental note of that."

I glance around the living area again. "Your apartment is gorgeous."

His eyes don't leave my face. "It's all right. You, on the other hand…"

His voice trails when there's a sudden, soft knock at the

door. "It's show time. Just so you know, I asked Mrs. Fields from the third floor to join in on the fun. She's a hoot."

I turn and watch as he approaches his apartment door. When it's opened, I spot Mrs. Sweeney with another gray-haired woman by her side. Both are sporting broad smiles on their faces.

Sean wraps his arms around them. "I'm a lucky bastard tonight. I get to spend time with the most beautiful women in this city."

They embrace him before the three of them part.

"Mrs. Fields, this is my new friend, Calliope." Sean steps aside to give me access to both women. "She lives next door to me."

"Calliope is a dream." Mrs. Sweeney reaches for my hand as I approach her. "She's one of the best neighbors I've ever had."

"Hey, now," Sean says in a low tone. "I'm standing right here."

Both women turn to glance at him, but it's Mrs. Sweeney who pats his cheek with her palm. "You're the best neighbor I've ever had, Sean. You're an incredibly special young man."

"You're one in a million," Mrs. Fields chimes in.

I silently agree with her. Sean Wells is definitely one in a million. I've never met a man quite like him before.

CHAPTER TWENTY-TWO

CALLIE

A RESTAURANT QUALITY DINNER, the best wine I've ever had, witty conversation, and he did the dishes on his own.

My boss is sliding up the perfect scale at breakneck speed.

"Sean is a magnificent cook, isn't he?" Mrs. Fields asks in a tone that is fueled by too much wine.

She practically screams the question out.

No one seems to notice since the Durkmans are engrossed in a conversation with Mrs. Sweeney about which variety of pear is the best.

That stems from the pear pie that Mr. Durkman presented for dessert. He wanted everyone at the table to believe that he spent the better part of the afternoon baking it.

He was completely oblivious to the fact that the bakery he bought it at stamps each of their foil pie plates with their logo.

As each piece was served, Mr. Durkman's dirty secret was revealed.

Not wanting to leave Mrs. Fields hanging, I answer her rhetorical question in my own way. "Dinner was delicious."

"He'll make someone a wonderful husband one day." She follows that with a wink that is sent in my direction.

I take a sip of the full-bodied red wine to save myself from responding to that. I'm not an expert, but if I had to guess the price of a bottle of this, it's more than my monthly salary.

The red wine selection at Tin Anchor is limited to three brands. Not one of them costs more than ten dollars a glass.

Sean strolls back into the dining room with a kitchen towel slung over his shoulder.

Every set of eyes in the room glances in his direction even though he hasn't said a word. I blame that on his magnetism. He commands attention whether he's speaking or not.

"How is it going in here?" He doesn't direct the question to anyone in particular.

"We're having a pear debate," Mrs. Sweeney offers. "Do you have a favorite pear, Sean?"

His gaze drops to the front of my dress. When it trails back up to my face, there's a smirk on his lips.

Is he insinuating that my tits are his favorite pair?

"I'm not a complicated man," he says as he sits next to me. "I prefer a nice juicy Bartlett. What about you, Calliope?"

"Bosc," I say without giving it a lot of thought. I follow that up with an explanation because I sense this crowd will want one. "I like how crisp they are."

Sean taps his forehead again. "Filed away for a rainy day."

"So, do tell." Mrs. Field leans an elbow on the table. "What's the story with you two?"

"Us?" I ask nervously.

Sean pats my hand. "Calliope not only lives next door to me, but she also works with me."

With, not for.

It's a distinction that I notice immediately.

I turn to look at him.

"Is that so?" Mrs. Sweeney's voice has a hint of amusement in it. "What a wonderful thing that is. My husband and I met on the job. Late husband. I still miss him."

I shift my gaze to her face, but there's no sorrow tainting her expression, just a soft smile.

"Is there an office romance brewing?" Mrs. Fields looks to Sean before her gaze jumps to me. "The chemistry between you two is at level two hundred on a scale of one to ten."

A nervous laugh falls from my lips. "No. Nothing like that. No office romance here."

Sean clears his throat, but I don't turn to look at him.

"Why not?" Mr. Durkman jumps into the discussion. "You're both young. You're both available, aren't you?"

"I am," Sean says before I can answer.

I drop my gaze to the linen cloth covering the table. "My last relationship ended not long ago. I'm still dealing with some things related to that."

"Understood," Mrs. Sweeney interrupts. "I remember those days when I was nursing a broken heart. Surround yourself with friends, Calliope. You have all of us, and Sean too. He's a great friend."

Nodding, I finally turn to look at my boss.

"I can't argue with that." His gaze drifts from Mrs. Sweeney to me. "I'm a hell of a good friend."

CHAPTER TWENTY-THREE

S<small>EAN</small>

MRS. SWEENEY just dropkicked me into the friend zone with Champ.

Who knew that hanging out with people who are old enough to be my grandparents would result in a very unwanted cock block?

Calliope's gaze drifts from my face back to the half-full wine glass on the table in front of her.

She's been slowly sipping at it all night, leaving behind the imprint of her soft pink lipstick against the rim of the glass.

I'm so infatuated with her that I'm tempted to keep it as it is for a few days so I can stare at it.

Jesus. I've got it bad for her.

I haven't crushed this hard on a woman in forever.

"I should call it a night." Mrs. Sweeney plants her hands on the top of the table to gain leverage to help her get out of my oversized dining room chairs.

They were a housewarming gift from my mother. The listing for them on the website she purchased them from should have come with an '*objects are much larger than their cited dimensions*' because they're as big as they are uncomfortable.

I would have sent all eight of the chairs back, but my mom insisted they fit the apartment's aesthetic.

Whatever the fuck that means.

I'll replace them soon with something more streamlined. I like simple and subtle when it comes to the interior of my home.

I'm out of my chair and heading over to Mrs. Sweeney in an instant.

I offer my hand. She takes it with a firm grip, using me as the leverage she needs to get to her feet.

"There wouldn't happen to be any leftovers, would there?" she quizzes with a bounce of both of her graying brows.

"I already packed it all up for you," I tell her. "I'll grab it before I walk you home."

"We'll walk her home." Mr. Durkman is on his feet, too, as is his wife.

Mrs. Fields downs what's left of the wine in her glass before she's up and ready to call it a night.

Calliope slowly stands too. "I'll go too."

"No," I spit out. "Hang out for a minute. I want to show you something."

It's my dick, but my respect for her and good old-fashioned manners won't allow me to whip it out when the coast is clear, so I smile.

"All right," Calliope says with just enough trepidation in her tone to suggest she might make a break for the door when she can.

I sprint to grab the leftovers before walking my guests to the door, chatting quietly with them about when we'll do this again.

I know that most of them have grandchildren they don't see often, so in a sense, I've stepped into that role for them. I've done that happily. I miss my grandparents. Two have died. The other two are off traveling the world, so my time with them is limited to video chats and phone calls.

As the door shuts behind my guests, I take a breath.

I'm alone at last with Calliope.

I start toward her, but the sound of my phone ringing stalls me.

"For fuck's sake," I mutter, making my way to where I left it on the dining room table.

Calliope laughs. "Something tells me that your work is never done."

"You've got that right," I say as I scoop up my phone and read the name on the screen. "It's Decky. He can go to hell."

I silence the ringing and look up to see Calliope smiling. "Why does your brother call you Saint?"

That's a lot to unpack, so I give her the condensed version. "My grandma first called me Saint because I was always the kid who helped out anyone who needed a hand. I outgrew the nickname, but Decky hasn't let it go."

She leans closer to me, tilting her chin up, so our eyes meet. "I think it suits you."

That is a compliment I don't deserve, so I divert. "Just like Champ suits you."

She gifts me a brilliant smile. "No one but you calls me that. I found that apron at a second-hand shop months ago. Everyone who works at the bar wears it."

"No one wears it better than you do." I look into her eyes. "Are you ready to see something spectacular?"

"I'm ready," she says.

I hold out a hand to her. "Come with me, Champ."

CHAPTER TWENTY-FOUR

Callie

I KNEW the building had amenities, but I didn't realize it had a magical garden in the form of a courtyard on the roof level.

The concrete beneath our feet is the only thing that isn't vibrant and welcoming.

Off-white furniture sits in one corner, a large grill is nearby, and a glass dining table complete with stunning high-backed white chairs is right in front of us.

Sprinkled throughout the space are flowering potted plants. It's all lit with soft lights set up in each corner.

I had no idea an oasis like this existed in the middle of this city.

I glance over my shoulder to see the door Sean just opened with a key.

Since Grady never mentioned this paradise, I don't know if he's aware it exists.

Curiosity pushes a question out of my mouth. "Only certain tenants have access to this, right?"

"That's right." Sean smiles. "Do you want access to it?"

I look around while envisioning sitting on the couch with a glass of wine in my hand while the sun is setting over the city on a warm evening. I could read a book up here on a lazy Saturday afternoon before grilling a steak and enjoying that with a salad for dinner.

The possibilities are endless.

I turn to face him. "Will it cost me?"

He takes a half step forward, so he's closer to me. "Yes."

Trepidation and excitement collide inside of me. Sean Wells is nothing like any man I've been involved with, but he's also my boss.

I push my reservations aside and decide to hear him out. "What's the price?"

"Dinner alone with me." He tilts his head slightly to the left. "No Delora. No one over the age of eighty."

A soft smile settles on my lips. "We work together."

I use his words from earlier against him as a reminder that we both have something to lose if this goes beyond where it is now.

I only started this job a few days ago, and I can already see a bright future at Wells.

He's the co-owner of the company. I imagine being involved with a subordinate would be a complication for him. He told me his brother is a hard-ass. I don't see him signing off on interoffice relationships.

"And?" Sean asks with a grin.

"And," I echo. "It must break some company policy."

"It doesn't."

I narrow my eyes as I study his face. "Your brother is fine with you going on a date with an employee?"

"Decky has done it in the past."

"Does that woman still work for Wells?" I question.

"All three of them still do," he quips.

Surprised by that, I take a step back. "What if we don't have fun when we're alone together?"

That lures a laugh from somewhere deep inside of him. "There is zero chance in hell that will happen. We're alone now, and I'm having a hell of a good time. Aren't you?"

I am, but I feel if I admit that, he'll take more pride in that than is warranted. He has to know he's incredibly fun to be around.

I suck in a breath. "This job is important to me. I know that I can contribute a lot to Wells. I don't want anything to get in the way of that. I really need this job."

He narrows the distance between us again with a forward step. "You have my word that wherever this goes, it has no bearing on your job. You report to Delora. Don't think for a moment that I would undermine that if you dump me after our first date."

"I might," I say teasingly.

"You won't," he counters with a smug grin.

That pushes me more. "How can you be so confident about that?"

His gaze trails over my face. "Whatever is happening between us is electric, Calliope. You feel it too. Don't fool yourself into thinking that one date with me will be enough."

Arrogance drips off this man, but it's intoxicating. He's intoxicating.

"What if I'm only looking for fun?" I ask him the question, even though I'm quizzing myself at the very same time.

I can't launch back into something serious, not after what happened between my ex and me. Dagen Hillstead wasn't the man I thought he was when I agreed to marry him. I let my guard down with him, and I'm still paying the price.

Sean's hand leaps to my chin. "You've come to the right place then."

I stare into his eyes and see sureness in them that I've never witnessed in a man's gaze before.

Warning flags are popping up all around me, but I ignore them all.

I deserve some fun, and who better to have it with than my hot-as-hell neighbor?

"Stop thinking about kissing me, Champ." His lips hover close to mine. "Bite the bullet and do it. I promise you won't regret it."

Something sparks deep inside of me when my lips touch his for the first time. I come alive. The cocoon I've built to shield myself in burns away from the searing heat of his kiss.

His hands jump to my back as I tangle my hands in his hair and lose myself to the moment and the magic of this place and him.

CHAPTER TWENTY-FIVE

Sean

WEALTH HAS AFFORDED me many things in life, but unfortunately, privacy at this moment, isn't one of them.

The sound of the door to the roof creaking open signals that someone else has decided to visit this slice of paradise in the big city tonight.

Champ's fingers leap to her lips as she stares at me with a look I can only describe as a combination of lust and panic.

I've seen that look on the face of women before, but that was years ago when I was a teenager. Nothing ruins the mood faster than getting caught kissing your girlfriend goodnight. That happened to me on more than one occasion. The most memorable time was when the girl's father was peering through their ground floor apartment window. He got an eyeful when my hand started inching down my girlfriend's back in search of her ass.

I never completed that journey because her dear old dad

chased me out of the neighborhood with a television remote in his hand.

I glance toward the door to see a couple that lives on the second floor. I smile as they approach us hand-in-hand.

"Sean." Cornell smiles. "Thank you again for the job."

I nod. "It's my pleasure."

Brandi lets out a sigh. "It's been a lifesaver. We had no idea what we'd do when his firm made cutbacks and let him go."

I turn to catch Calliope's gaze centered on my face.

"I'm Brandi, and this is my husband Cornell." Brandi extends a hand to Champ. "We're Sean's neighbors."

"You're Calliope's neighbors too." I step in to make the introductions as they exchange a handshake. "She's living in her brother's apartment for a few months. It's next door to mine."

Brandi's blonde hair whips to the side as she turns to face me. "Isn't that nice?"

I know that tone.

These two incredible people have been trying to set me up since they moved into the building. I've sidestepped every potential date with the excuse that I'm buried in work.

"We work together," Champ offers. "I work at Wells."

Cornell glances at me before his gaze settles on Champ's face. "I do too. I started in their legal department a couple of weeks ago."

Calliope's face lights up. "I thought you looked familiar. You came into Tin Anchor with Sean and Declan for a mid-day drink one day, didn't you?"

Cornell nods. "My first day on the job. The brothers took me out for a celebratory drink. You served us, didn't you? So you work at the bar and Wells?"

"I do," she affirms with a grin.

Brandi takes a step toward us. "You two should join us for dinner one night. Our two-year-old son, Lee, loves having someone new to play with, especially pretty girls."

Calliope laughs. "Why don't the three of you come to my apartment for dinner one night? I'll invite the Durkmans, Mrs. Sweeney, and Mrs. Fields too."

I tap her shoulder. "And?"

The smile she shoots in my direction could light up this entire city on the darkest night of the year. "And you too, Sean."

"I'm there," I say before anyone else can get a word in. "Name the day and time. I'll be there."

We lock eyes before she turns back to Cornell and Brandi. "It was nice to meet you both. I can't tell you how much I'm looking forward to meeting little Lee."

"We'd go grab him now for a meet and greet, but he's fast asleep. My mom is in town for a few days, so she's standing guard over him." Brandi smiles as she tugs a phone out of the back pocket of her jeans. "Let's exchange numbers, Calliope."

Calliope calls out her number.

If I hadn't already looked it up in her employment file and added it to my phone's contact list, I'd be doing that now.

"I'm going to call it a night," Calliope says.

Since her keys are in one of the pockets of her dress, there's no reason for her to go back to my apartment with me.

I reach out to catch her hand in mine. Not caring what anyone thinks, I bring it to my lips and plant a series of soft kisses on her fingertips. "Goodnight, Calliope."

She stares into my eyes, studying me. Likely, trying to gauge what I'm thinking.

I wish I knew.

All I know for sure is that I'm looking forward to

standing next to her on the sidewalk in the morning before we go to work.

I could look at her every day for the rest of my life, and each time, I'd see something in her eyes or something written within her expression that is new to me.

"Goodnight, Sean," she whispers before she turns to walk away.

I keep my gaze trained on her until she disappears behind the door.

"Sean." Brandi edges a fingertip into my shoulder. "That was fire. The way you kissed her hand, and oh my god, how she looked at you."

"It's how we looked at each other on our first date," Cornell says, wrapping an arm around his wife's waist.

"She's…" My voice trails because I don't have words.

I'm fucking tongue-tied after kissing Calliope.

"Yes, she is." Brandi laughs. "I think we are witnessing the downfall of one of New York City's most eligible bachelors."

"That we are," Cornell agrees with a curt nod. "Sean Wells just had his heart stolen."

I laugh that off, patting the center of my chest as I do. "My heart is right here."

They smile in a way that tells me they know I'm bullshitting them.

I'm far from being head over heels in love with Calliope, but that kiss wasn't like anything I've experienced.

I'm craving more, so tomorrow morning, I plan on firming up a dinner date with my neighbor, so I can end the night with another kiss that rivals our first.

CHAPTER TWENTY-SIX

CALLIE

"OF COURSE, I'LL DO IT," I say into my phone as I wait on the sidewalk in front of my building for Jurgen to arrive.

Sean is nowhere in sight. I feel a slight sense of relief from that.

Our kiss last night kept me awake for hours.

It was brief, and I craved more, but it set the tone for what might be waiting for me in the future.

If a man can kiss like that, what's he capable of in bed?

"You're my hero, Callie." Naomi sighs. "Harlan will do a naked cartwheel when he finds out what I have planned for him."

I don't want any of those details, so I push the conversation forward by asking a crucial question. "Do you need me to pick up dinner for the kids on my way to your place, or…"

"That would be a dream come true," my sister interrupts me. "Chicken nuggets and fries always top their lists."

That's as easy as easy can be.

"When these concert tickets landed in my lap this morning, I couldn't believe it," she explains again why she needs a last minute sitter for tonight. "I asked the kids who they wanted to watch over them, and you won by a landslide."

I'd call her out on that lie, but it won't serve any purpose other than embarrassing her.

My mom texted me a heads-up just before my phone rang five minutes ago.

Naomi had asked her and my dad to watch Bodhi and Tabitha tonight, but they already had plans.

I don't mind being second choice.

"Champ!"

I turn and raise a hand in greeting when I hear Sean call out my nickname.

When he spots the phone in my hand, his index finger darts to his lips as if he's silencing himself.

"I'll come to your place right after work," I tell Naomi in an effort to wrap up the call. "If you need me to bring anything else, shoot me a text message."

"Thank you!" she sing-songs into my ear. "Try not to stare at your boss all day."

I feel my cheeks redden just as I end the call.

Sean dips his head to get a better look when I drop my gaze to the ground. "Are you blushing, Calliope?"

"No," I murmur. "It's warm out this morning."

Naturally, the wind whips past us at the worst possible moment sending a few strands of my hair into my face.

I reach up to hold it in place as another gust follows.

"It's brisk," he says with a chuckle. "Sounds like I'm going to be turned down if I ask you out to dinner tonight."

Convinced that the blush on my cheeks has faded, I look up to see him staring at me. "I have plans."

"At someone's place," he adds.

I know a fishing expedition when it's happening in plain sight.

"That's right." I nod.

His gaze slides over the light blue pencil skirt I'm wearing. "Is there a chance you'll come home tonight with another work of art on your ass?"

I look past him to see Jurgen on the approach behind the wheel of the SUV. "There's a very good chance that will happen."

His gaze never leaves my face. "Looks like I'll be camping out in the lobby tonight, considering I'm an art connoisseur."

I laugh. "I know you spy on me through the peephole in your door, so you can skip the lobby."

"You only know that because you do the same thing," he counters.

I take a step forward. "Our ride is here."

His hand reaches out to grab my elbow to stop me in place. "I want to clear something up, Champ. The other day…that woman you saw at my door, nothing happened there. She lost an earring at the party. I found it and sent her on her way."

I appreciate the explanation, but he doesn't owe me that. He doesn't owe me anything. We haven't even gone on our first date yet, so discussing other people we may or may not be interested in is premature.

I can't allow myself to fall too deep, too fast. I have to keep my wits about me if I want to balance my job and whatever is happening between us.

"I'm sure she appreciated your help, Sean."

He offers me a grin in response.

I don't wait for him to add anything to that. I climb into the car once Jurgen opens the back passenger door. By the time Sean is next to me, his phone is at his ear as he answers an incoming call from what sounds like one of the company's distribution managers.

As the driver steers the car back into traffic, I keep my gaze trained on the street.

Whenever I'm within a few feet of my boss, the intensity in the air between us is impossible to ignore.

If it feels like this after just one kiss, what in the hell will it be like after we've spent a night together?

CHAPTER TWENTY-SEVEN

Sean

I READ the list of marketing ideas for the winter campaign that Delora shoved in my hand two minutes ago. I spot one idea with limited promise but beyond that bland is the standard she seems to be shooting for.

"Very funny." I toss the piece of paper with notes for the lackluster ideas on my desk. "Give me the real list now."

To accentuate that point, I hold out my empty palm.

Delora's gaze drops to the paper on my desk. "That was it."

My jaw twitches at that admission. "This isn't funny, Delora."

Her hands drop to her hips. "It's not supposed to be, Sean. I think every single idea on that list is a winner."

I push back from my desk to stand so we're almost eye-to-eye since she refused to take a seat when she arrived at my office door.

That makes sense now. She likely wanted to leave the option open to make a quick getaway after she presented that bullshit to me.

"If that's a true statement, you're fired."

Her eyes go as wide as saucers. "Very funny."

I'd give her credit for using my words against me, but I'm not in a jovial mood at the moment. Declan already dropped one problem in my lap when he shot out of the door to head to a meeting uptown.

I put that fire out, but I'm still tempted to overhaul our inventory control department.

All of their records may as well be in another language since I can't decipher them.

If only Declan would have taken my advice and not hired three of his friends from middle school to man that department. I'm not convinced that any of them have the ability to count.

In times like this, I think my brother should have used his law degree in the spirit in which he earned it by defending criminals or prosecuting them.

Roping him into this business seemed like a bright idea at the time.

"Who came up with that shit?" I ask with exasperation evident in my tone.

The question stems from a place of genuine curiosity because the entire marketing department might find themselves in the same line at the unemployment office as the inventory control department. Or maybe, I just switch them out and give them a chance to handle a set of new tasks.

I laugh inwardly at the potential marketing ideas Declan's friends would come up with.

"All of us," Delora admits. "Every person has at least one contribution on that list."

If that's true, Champ has let me down.

I snatch the paper up again and scan it. Even with a second read through, nothing jumps out at me. "This is every idea that your department came up with?"

"Not every idea," she admits. "There was one that didn't make the list."

"You're holding back, Delora." I drop back into my chair. "Tell me about that one."

"It's a yearly subscription as a holiday gift."

With my interest piqued, I roll my hand. "I need to hear more than that."

Delora laughs. "It's a crazy idea. That's why I didn't mark it down. Who in their right mind would pay a fee to get a new pair of underwear delivered to someone else's door once a month? We'd have to lower the price of our products to appeal to a bigger demographic."

"You don't believe that's achievable?"

"I don't believe it's a worthwhile gamble," she clarifies. "That's why I didn't include it on the list. I told Callie to come up with something different to present to you."

"The subscription idea came from Calliope?"

She nods. "You know how it is with new hires, Sean. It's hard to balance their enthusiasm with reality."

I drop my gaze back to the list of bullshit ideas before leaning back in my chair. "Flesh the subscription model out more. I want you to have a full presentation ready by mid-month."

"Sean." My name snaps off her tongue.

"Delora." I mimic her tone. "Put your all into this."

She shakes her head. "All right. You're the boss."

I am, and I don't know if I'm seeing potential in this because Champ is the mastermind behind it, but I want to learn more. Not just about the campaign idea but the woman responsible for it.

I'M a man who sticks to his word.

If I make a promise, you can bet everything you own that I will follow through with it.

That's why I'm in the lobby of my building with a book in hand.

I don't know what it's about. I plucked it out of a shelf in the extra bedroom in my apartment two hours ago. Declan supplied the books and the shelf as a housewarming gift.

Leave it to my older brother to choose something that I have zero interest in.

I could have camped out here in the corner in this uncomfortable armchair with my phone or laptop, but even I need a break from business sometimes.

I anticipated that Calliope would be home by now. It's nearing eleven. The last time she hung out with the tiny artist, she was back home by nine.

I look up when I hear the unmistakable scuff of Lester's shoes against the polished marble floor as he heads toward the building's entrance.

My patience pays off when he swings open the door, and utter perfection walks into the lobby wearing the same black blouse and light blue skirt she had on this morning.

Champ shoots the doorman a smile that could warm the coldest heart.

They exchange words that I'm too far away to hear, but it ends with her handing him a bill from her purse. From where I'm standing, it looks like a five.

Generosity is never about the size of the gift but the intention behind it.

She values people.

I've seen that both times we've shared dinner with our neighbors.

She leaves Lester with another smile before she sets off toward the elevator.

I stay in place, watching her graceful movements as her hair skips over her shoulders with each forward step. Her tits bounce within the confines of her bra beneath her blouse. Her hips sway.

She's incredibly sensual, even like this after a full day of work and what I imagine to be a spirited evening with her niece.

My gaze trails her as she nears the elevator. Her ass is spectacular under her skirt. There are no remnants of a wayward art project tonight.

I approach her from behind with unhurried steps.

When I'm within two feet of her, she gazes over her shoulder.

The smile I get rivals the one she just gave Lester. "Hey, Saint."

"Champ," I say as I take a spot next to her. "How was your evening?"

"Any evening spent with my niece and nephew is always great."

I barely register the fact that she confessed that she has a nephew as well as an artistic niece. I can't focus on anything but the way her cheeks are slowly turning pink.

Her gaze drops to the book in my hand. "Did you just get home? Were you at book club?"

I laugh that off. "I have no fucking idea what that is, so

no. I've been sitting in the lobby all night. I was waiting for you."

Her blue eyes widen beneath her long dark lashes. "You were? Why?"

The elevator's door slide open, so I motion for her to board it. "I wanted to walk you home."

CHAPTER TWENTY-EIGHT

CALLIE

OUR CONVERSATION in the elevator consisted of the plot of the thriller in Sean's hand. I've heard about the book, but until today, I hadn't considered reading it.

I don't know if my sudden interest in what some reviewers have labeled a '*high-paced novel with twists and turns for the ages*' is based on my love of reading or if I'm trying to avoid a more intimate discussion with my neighbor.

As I rattled on about the potential spoilers I had read online about the book, Sean kept his gaze locked on my face.

I step off the elevator with my boss by my side.

His hand grazes my back as we start toward my apartment door.

What am I supposed to do now? Do I invite him in? Strip him down to his underwear? Is this where I get to fulfill all of my most recent fantasies?

"You're blushing, Champ," he points out.

Dammit.

I skim a hand over my left cheek. "I walked from the subway. I guess I got a bit overheated."

His left brow cocks. "You weren't blushing in the elevator."

Of course he'd notice that.

I laugh it off. "It's warm on our floor, isn't it? Maybe we need to call maintenance."

"Maybe you're thinking about kissing me again."

I drop my gaze to the floor. "Maybe I'm not."

His fingers find my chin to lure it up until our eyes lock. "I'm thinking about kissing you again."

My gaze trails over every inch of his handsome face before I stop to stare at his lips. "You are?"

"I've been thinking about it all day."

I take a half-step back, hoping I'll find my common sense there because every cell in my body is screaming at me to invite him into my apartment.

A smile coasts over his lips. "I had an ulterior motive for wanting to walk you home tonight."

Hope flutters in the base of my belly. Is he about to tell me he wants to come into my apartment?

"What motive?" I ask quietly.

"I want to officially ask you out for our first date." He tucks the book under his arm. "Dinner, maybe some dancing, or bowling if you'd prefer."

I laugh. "Bowling?"

"Options are always a good thing." He lifts his chin. "Are you free tomorrow night?"

This is really happening. My boss is asking me out.

I nod. "I'm free."

"Do I need to dig my bowling shoes out of my storage locker, or will dinner at Nova suffice?"

Nova is one of the most popular restaurants in the city.

I glance down. "The shoes you're wearing will do just fine."

"Nova it is." He tugs the book out from under his arm. "It seems to me that you're pretty interested in this. Why don't you give it a read?"

I take the offered book. "Thank you. I'll return it as soon as I'm done."

"No rush." He smiles. "I don't charge late fees."

A soft noise coming from behind Mrs. Sweeney's door sends our gazes in that direction.

"Let's save our next kiss for after our first date," Sean whispers. "I wouldn't want Mrs. Sweeney to get jealous."

A soft chuckle escapes me. "Do you two have something going on?"

He nods curtly. "I sometimes take her to the roof for a glass of wine and a cigar while we star gaze."

"You smoke the cigar while she drinks the wine?"

"She indulges in both," he says. "As do I."

"You're a charmer," I accuse with a laugh. "You charm everyone you meet, don't you?"

"Have I charmed you, Champ?"

I hold up my hand with my index finger and thumb no more than an inch apart. "Just a little bit."

He scoops my hand in his before he kisses my palm. "I need to work harder then. Goodnight, Calliope."

"Goodnight, Saint."

My hand falls from his grasp, and with one brief last look at me, he walks to his door, unlocks it, and disappears inside his apartment.

———

AN HOUR LATER, I finally settle into a big armchair in the corner of Grady's guestroom to prepare myself for an hour-long reading session before I go to bed.

I've been soaking in the bathtub since I got home.

When I lived with my friends, we didn't have a tub.

We had one narrow shower.

I didn't enjoy my time in it. It was more of a get in and get out situation, but tonight I poured myself a glass of sparkling raspberry water, lit a candle, and used a few drops of the soothing lavender bubble bath Naomi bought me last month as a thank you gift for helping with her kids.

She did that in anticipation of me moving in here since she clearly remembered how I'd spend hours in the bathtub when we were growing up.

As I flip open the book's cover to dive into the first page, my phone chimes.

Grumbling, I get up and walk toward where I plugged it in to charge on the nightstand.

Sitting down on the bed dressed only in my panties and a tank top, I smile when I see a notification flash on the screen of an incoming text message.

Unknown: *Have you read any good books lately, Champ?*

Before responding, I add the number to my contact list along with Sean's name.

Callie: *Do you mean have I read any good books since I last saw you?*

His reply is instant.

Sean: *Let's go with that.*

Laughing, I type out a response and hit send.

Callie: *I was just about to start reading. I spent the last hour soaking in the tub.*

A sudden loud bang causes me to jolt. My phone teeters in my hand. Before I can get up to investigate if something has fallen, another message pops onto my screen.

Sean: *Don't panic, Champ. Nothing broke. No one is trying to break in.*

With shaking hands, I punch out a reply.

Callie: *You heard that too? Are you sure it's nothing?*

I read his response the moment it hits my phone's screen.

Sean: *That thud was me passing out when you said you were in the tub. The only thing separating your naked body from my eyes is a wall.*

I laugh so loud that I'm sure he can hear me.

Sean: *Don't stay up all night reading.*

I reply quickly.

Callie: *I won't. I'll see you in the morning.*

CHAPTER TWENTY-NINE

Sean

I TAKE my time when I exit the elevator because Calliope is waiting for Jurgen in the lobby today. The pouring rain must have chased her back into the shelter of the building.

I can tell she tried to tough it out because from where I'm standing, a few strands of her dampened hair are clinging to her cheek, and more distractingly, her black blouse is wet.

It's clear from this vantage point that she's wearing a red bra underneath.

Suddenly, she turns slightly, and her eyes lock on mine.

Panic darts over her expression.

I up the pace of my steps because if she's in need, I'm the man for the job.

"I'm a mess," she says, her cheeks turning the same shade of pink that they always do when I'm within ten feet of her.

Am I the reason she blushes?

Does this gorgeous, accomplished, smart-as-a-whip woman have it as bad for me as I do for her?

"You're beautiful," I tell her, and I fucking mean it.

I don't care that she looks like she just washed ashore on a deserted island.

She's gorgeous.

She points at the glass doors of the lobby. "Mrs. Fields had to leave for an appointment. Lester went to look for an umbrella, but Mrs. Fields insisted on going out in the rain because her ride was waiting. It took her a minute to get into the car, so I stood there helping her. The damn driver didn't even get out to lend a hand… and well, this happened."

This.

I assume she's referring to her sensual, slightly wet look.

"You look amazing."

Her brows bunch together. "I'm a soaked mess."

I glance over her shoulder to see Jurgen parking my car next to the curb. A quick look at my watch confirms the time.

It's twenty minutes to nine.

Calliope steals a peek behind her. "Dammit. I don't have time to clean up. I have to go to work looking like this."

My opportunity to give her what she needs falls directly into my lap.

"Head up to your apartment." I smile. "Jurgen will drive me to work, then circle back to get you."

"Decky will be mad if I'm late. I can't risk my job over something like this."

The effortless way she calls my brother by his nickname warms my heart.

I laugh. "I'll handle him. Take your time. No rush."

Relief floods her expression. "Do you mean it?"

"I mean it."

She inches up on her tiptoes to plant a soft kiss on my cheek. "You really are a saint."

I'm a sinner, but she's not aware of that quite yet.

Before I let her race to the elevator, I catch her forearm in my hand to hold her in place.

My gaze drops to the front of her blouse and the unmistakable outline of her pert little nipples under her bra.

When I look at her face again, the blush on her cheeks has darkened.

"I won't be riding home with you after work." I stare into her brilliant blue eyes. "I will be at your door at eight to take you to dinner, Calliope."

"Okay," she whispers. "Eight for our date."

I lean forward so my breath skirts over the skin of her neck. "I'll be counting every fucking minute until then."

"Me too." Her voice comes out ragged and edged with the same need that is brewing inside of me.

Loosening my grip on her, I kiss her forehead. "Have a good day, Champ."

Her eyes trail up my body to my face. "You too, Saint."

I'M AT IT AGAIN.

Fishing in unchartered waters.

I've plugged Calliope's name into Google in every manner that I can think of.

Calliope Morrow.

Callie Morrow.

Callie from Tin Anchor.

I even spent the better part of an hour perusing every fucking hashtag that has anything to do with that bar she works at.

I was hoping to land a big catch in the form of a clue about her life.

When I saw her this morning, looking both sexy-as-fuck,

and vulnerable-as-hell in the lobby, I had a sudden urge to protect her.

I know that whatever happened in her last relationship scarred her, so I want any scrap of information that will tell me more about that and who the hell the idiot was that let her slip out of his grasp.

I look up from my computer screen when I hear Decky clearing his throat.

"Knock," I tell him. "Just goddamn knock if you want to talk to me."

His hand glides down the front of his neck. "Not everything is about you, Saint. I took a bite of a bagel that got caught between here and there."

"Do you need me to do the Heimlich?"

A bark of laughter follows a cough. "I'm fine. The last time you tried to administer first aid, you broke one of my ribs."

"I was twelve," I point out. "I hadn't gotten first aid training yet."

He takes a full step into my office. "And you have now?"

I tap the corner of my laptop screen. "I've watched a few videos. I'm confident I can save you without breaking anything."

"I'll pass." His arms cross over his chest. "Do you want to meet up tonight? There's a new restaurant opening in Tribeca. I scored a couple of invites to their soft launch."

"I can't," I say directly. "I'm taking Calliope out for dinner."

His brow furrows. "Really?"

"Really," I echo. "I like her."

It's an admission I didn't have to make, but I know my brother. He'll probe and prod until I tell him how I feel about my neighbor. Tossing him a crumb will satisfy him for now.

"Look at you crushing on a girl." He laughs before he quickly corrects himself. "On a woman."

"She's an incredible woman," I stress his point. "Intelligent, kind, and she thinks I'm charming."

His smile carries to his eyes. "Try not to mess it up, Saint."

"I won't," I say with conviction. "I'll do everything within my power to not fuck this up."

CHAPTER THIRTY

CALLIE

I GLANCE at the young couple sitting at the table near us. "Do you think they're on their first date too?"

Sean's gaze doesn't leave my face. "Absolutely."

I let out a stuttered laugh. "You didn't even look at who I'm referring to."

His head shakes slightly. "I don't need to. I saw them when they first arrived. She's blonde with black-rimmed glasses. A pink hair tie is wrapped around her ponytail. He's sporting the beginnings of a mustache. His hands are shaking like we're in the middle of a magnitude six point nine quake."

I steal a glance to see the dark-haired guy's hands quivering as he reaches for his water glass.

"It's about to get a lot more relaxed over there," Sean comments.

My gaze drifts back to his face. "How so?"

He leans forward. "I ordered them a bottle of champagne. A few sips of that, and those first date nerves will disappear."

My eyes widen. "When did you order them champagne?"

"When you were in the washroom trying to chase away that blush on your cheeks."

I dip my chin to hide the sudden rush of heat I feel.

"Champ," Sean says my name softly.

I glance up. "What?"

"Tell me about your first date."

That's completely unexpected, but it beats talking about my reddened cheeks, so I'm all in. "I was in eighth grade, I think. We went out for burgers. My oldest brother chaperoned."

"How were the burgers?"

I laugh. "Fine. Why?"

"You can tell a lot about a man from his restaurant choices." He glances around us. "I would have brought you to a place like this for dinner when you were in eighth grade."

Shaking my head, I smile. "You would have been too old for me then."

"I'm twenty-nine, Calliope."

"I'm twenty-five," I point out. "When I was in eighth grade, you were…"

"Too old for you." His brow perks. "Let's talk about first kisses."

Our waiter interrupts us. He arrives with a tablet in hand and what seems to be a rehearsed speech about the specials for the night.

I order salmon. Sean chooses a steak, rare and a bottle of wine that will compliment both of our meals.

Once the waiter has wandered off, I take control of the conversation. "Do you remember your first kiss?"

Sean tugs on the lapels of his dark blue suit jacket.

He looks incredible tonight. The white button-down shirt he's wearing is a perfect canvas for his violet striped tie.

I opted for a dress in almost the same hue.

We shared a laugh on our way here about how color coordinated we are.

"I remember it not-so-fondly," he admits. "Promise me you're not going to laugh."

"I can't promise that," I say honestly.

"Promise you won't laugh too loud," he counters.

"Promise."

"I was a late comer to the first kiss party." He chuckles. "I was thirteen and thought I had the perfect candidate in mind."

"Who?" I blurt out.

"Savannah Atteridge," he says softly. "My best friend."

A smile blooms on my lips. "How did your first kiss with Savannah Atteridge go?"

"Horribly."

I hold in a laugh. "Why?"

"My grandparents had a swimming pool on the roof of their building," he begins before taking a sip from the water glass in front of him. "I invited Savi to swim because she was a champion. She had literally won medals for swimming, and I thought she'd appreciate the extra pool time."

"That was nice of you," I say.

"I jumped into the deep end." He shakes his head. "Didn't realize it was the deep end, mind you, and I had no fucking idea how to swim."

My hand jumps to my mouth. "Oh no."

"Oh no is right." He smirks. "Savi dove in to save me. Somehow she dragged me to the edge, and I saw it as an opportunity to get her lips on mine, so I played the semi-drowning victim and kept my eyes closed."

"You didn't."

"I sure as hell did." He sighs. "She pushed my chest a few

times for good measure, lined her lips up with mine, and *boom* moved in for the mouth-to-mouth save."

Mesmerized by this story, I lean an elbow on the table and focus on his face. "What happened next?"

His tongue darts out to slick his bottom lip. "I wrapped a hand around the back of her neck and held her in place for what I thought would be the best first kiss ever."

"Was she receptive?"

A bark of a laugh flows from him. "Hell no she wasn't. She punched me in the chest and got up to walk away."

I glance to the left when I see the waiter approaching with a bottle of wine in his hand. "Did that ruin your friendship?"

"Not a chance," he says. "Two minutes after she punched me, she apologized and told me it wasn't me. According to her, I wasn't the worst kisser in the world."

I can vouch for that too, but I keep that to myself. "Did you ever try and kiss her again?"

"No." He spots the waiter as he nears our table, but before he gives his attention to him, he smiles at me. "Not long after that, Savi told me that she liked kissing girls as much as I did. I was the first person she told that to."

That doesn't surprise me. There's something about him that is disarming. I can see why people would want to confide in him.

A part of me wants to do that as well, but I don't know if I ever will.

CHAPTER THIRTY-ONE

S<small>EAN</small>

"ARE YOU AND SAVANNAH STILL FRIENDS?" Champ asks as we exit the car in front of our building.

Dinner was magnificent.

The food was decadent, the wine just as delicious, and the company was the best I've ever had.

Our conversation ranged from our first kisses to our impressions of growing up in New York.

Calliope has spent all of her life here, working her way through the public school system as well as gracing the halls of NYU with her presence.

Private school was where I began my educational journey, but when I was kicked out in the fourth grade, my dad won the battle of letting me attend public school. I did that until I graduated eighth grade. After that, I was sent upstate to The Buchanan School to follow in my maternal grandfather's footsteps.

A couple of years spent at Brown University followed that.

"We are," I tell her. "We don't talk as much as we used to. Savi lives in Minneapolis now. She and her wife adopted twin boys three years ago."

She says goodnight to Jurgen before she turns to face me. "It's nice that you're still in contact with each other."

I motion for her to approach the lobby doors. "Do you still keep in touch with your friends from when you were a kid?"

"No," she says softly. "We all drifted apart."

That's a shame.

I'm fortunate in the fact that I have several close friends. I've never taken that for granted.

Lester swings open the door. I tuck a few twenties in his palm as I pass him.

His whispered thank you earns a smile from me.

He may be an expert at putting himself in the right place at the right time to earn a generous tip, but he's intuitive enough to know when not to inject himself in the middle of a conversation.

"I consider my sister my closest friend," Calliope admits as we near the bank of elevators. "She's a few years older than me. I love hanging out with her and her kids."

"Including the burgeoning artist with the tiny hands."

She laughs. "Tabitha. Her name is Tabitha. Bodhi is my nephew, and there's another baby on the way."

"Three kids?" I raise three fingers on my right hand to punctuate the question.

She nods. "I doubt she'll stop there."

As the elevator doors slide open, I take her hand in mine. "I bet you're the best aunt in this city."

Her gaze trails from our joined hands to my face. "I try to

be. Are you an uncle? Does Declan have kids? Do you have other siblings?"

"As far as I know, I'm not an uncle," I murmur as I tap the button on the panel for our floor. "There's Decky, me, and Ava. She's twenty. Living her best life in London at the moment."

She squeezes my hand. "Is Ava anything like you or Decky?"

"No." I chuckle. "She's innocent and wants nothing to do with men's underwear. At least I hope to hell she doesn't because she's way too young to be thinking about that."

"Newsflash, Saint." She gazes up at me. "Twenty-year-old women aren't too young to be thinking about men in their underwear or out of it."

"Quiet down, Champ." I plant a soft kiss on her mouth to shush her. "The only thing I want to talk about for the rest of this date is you."

Her gaze lingers on my lips. "Our date isn't over yet?"

I kiss her palm as the elevator signals its arrival on our floor. "Not by a long shot."

———

WE'RE ON THE ROOF.

I planned on taking Calliope to my apartment, but I could feel her hand shaking in mine when we rode the elevator up to our floor.

I want this woman more than I've wanted anyone in my life, but there's no way in hell I'm going to rush her.

I still don't have any sense of what happened in her last relationship, so I want to tread carefully.

She's not looking for anything serious. I can't say I am

either, but I want our time together to be a good experience for her.

"Are you scared of heights, Champ?"

Her gaze floats past my shoulder to the lights of the city beyond. From this vantage point, it looks like they go on forever.

She laughs a little. "Why would you ask me that?"

"Why would you answer the question with another question?"

She mumbles something I can't quite make out, so I close the distance between us with a few steps.

"I didn't quite get that," I say, cupping a hand over my ear.

"I like the view from right here." She points to the concrete beneath her feet. "Why wander that close to the edge?"

"Because the glass that borders it is a reminder that the edge is a dangerous place." I hold out a hand to her. "You can come closer to get the full view. Right now, you're only enjoying part of it."

With a slight bit of noticeable hesitation, she drops her hand in mine. "Do you like being close to the edge, Saint?"

"We only live once, so I want to experience as much possible." I squeeze her hand. "If that means taking chances sometimes, I'm all in."

Her gaze creeps up my chest until our eyes lock. "Taking a chance is harder for some people than others."

We've wandered away from discussing the edge of the roof. She's dipping a toe into something far more personal than that, so I tread lightly. "Is it harder for you, Calliope?"

Her chin bobs up and down.

"Because of your ex-fiancé?"

I half expect her to bolt toward the door, but she stands her ground. "Yes."

"You're scared to take a chance with me," I state.

It's not a question. I see the trepidation in her expression. I feel it in the slight tremor in her hand.

"I was engaged to a man like you." Her hand shakes. "He wasn't exactly like you, but he was wealthy."

"One billionaire is not the same as another."

That brings a smile to her full lips. "He's a millionaire."

I swear I feel my chest puff out at that proclamation. I've never compared myself to other men, but I want to be a better man in every sense than the asshole she almost married.

"I don't know what the fuck he did to mess things up with you, but I'm telling you right now that I'm an honest bastard. I won't string you along or play any games with you." I reach to cup her cheeks in my hands. "We've established that we're both looking for fun, so let's have some. No expectations. No bullshit. Just two adults doing what they do best."

"Doing what they do best?" she echoes, trying to push back a smile.

"I'm great in bed," I admit. "Something tells me we have that in common."

Her gaze trails me from head to toe and then back up again. "Something tells me that you're better than great."

I lean down to press a kiss to her mouth. "When you're ready to find out, say the word. I'm yours for the taking, Calliope."

"When I'm ready, I'll say the word," she whispers.

I take her mouth again, but this time I'm greedy. The kiss is slow, intense, and driven by my desperate need to prove how much I want her.

"Okay," she says the moment our lips part. "I'm saying

the word. Or I will on Friday. Maybe we can hang out after work. Do you want to have dinner together again?"

I want to dine on her body now, but I can wait if this is what she needs.

Brushing a strand of her hair from her forehead, I stare into the depths of her beautiful blue eyes. "I want that very much."

Her face lights up. "I'll choose the place. It'll be my treat."

"No." I shake my head. "You choose, and it's my treat."

She scratches the side of her neck. "I want to treat you."

I can tell it's important to her, so I nod. "You'll treat me."

"I will." She gazes past me to the city beyond. "Will you walk me home now, Saint?"

A smile coasts over my lips. "That would be my pleasure."

CHAPTER THIRTY-TWO

Callie

"GREAT NEWS, CALLIE!"

Before I even turn to look at Delora, I know she's smiling. I can hear it in her voice. We haven't worked together for very long, but her moods are telling.

She spent most of yesterday in her office with the door closed. The scowl on her face was evident through the glass wall that gives her unfettered visual access to my co-workers and me.

I spin in my office chair to see her approaching my cubicle. "What's the news?"

I'm about to glide to my feet, but her hand movement indicates that she wants me to stay put. She backs that up with the next words out of her mouth. "Don't get up on my account. I want you at your desk, working, so you're exactly where you need to be."

I huff out a laugh. "I've been sprucing up our socials. I'm not sure if you've had a chance to take a peek at those yet."

She sighs. "I will. I've been preoccupied. Larry and I hit a speed bump yesterday, but we're back on track today. Right now, I want to talk about your idea for the winter marketing campaign."

I tossed a few ideas out for that. She didn't seem particularly receptive to any of them.

"The subscription idea caught Sean's attention," she says. "He wants us to pull together a presentation for him. I know him well enough to know that he's looking for more than mock-up marketing materials. He expects projections including customer acquisition costs and potential sales numbers."

"Wow." That one word leaves my lips because I'm stunned.

"I've been working on this myself to develop a roadmap for us to move forward with." She offers me a half-smile. "I'll admit that I had reservations about it, but I've done some research, and I see that it's a model that has proven profitable for other companies."

I take pride in knowing that she and Sean see the merit in my idea.

"I'll get to work on this right away," I say with butterflies in my stomach.

This is my first real chance to prove myself to not only Delora but Declan and Sean too.

"Let's grab lunch in an hour to hatch a plan." She glances to where my co-workers are sitting in their cubicles. "Justin and Rory will join us. It's all hands on deck for this."

Justin and Rory have been wonderful to me since I started working here. They've answered every question I've had and have shown me nothing but patience and respect.

I'm excited to dive into this with them by my side.

"Does that sound good to you?" Delora asks, her gaze

dropping to the black blouse and pants I'm wearing. "I'll call ahead to make sure the restaurant has room to seat the four of us. How does Italian food sound?"

"Delicious." I smile.

"Perfect." She gestures toward her office. "We'll eat while we hammer out a strategy to conquer this project. We're going to blow Sean away with this."

That's exactly what I plan on doing.

I GLANCE to where Sean is sitting on the seat next to me.

There's something alluring about every part of him, including his hands. Both are resting on his thighs as Jurgen steers the car through the early evening Manhattan traffic as we make the trek home.

"What's on your mind, Champ?"

My gaze jumps from his hands to his face. "What? Nothing. Why would you think there's something on my mind?"

A low chuckle falls from his lips. "That right there cemented it. It was a simple question, not an inquisition."

Smiling, I look down at my lap. "I need to thank you."

"For smelling this good?" He cocks a brow. "I'm still wearing that Matiz cologne you like. I may never switch brands."

He does smell good. I know it can't all be attributed to the cologne. I imagine he smells sinful even when he steps out of the shower.

My mind conjures up an image of what that must look like. I already can envision it from the waist up since I got a glimpse of him shirtless that night the blonde woman knocked on his door.

"What do you think you need to thank me for, Calliope?"

His deep voice lures my gaze back up to meet his. "For having faith in my idea. Delora told me today that you're interested in hearing more about the subscription model proposal."

His hand jumps to rub his jaw. "I think there's potential there. I'm interested in seeing more details. I don't want you to have false hope, though. We won't run with this until I'm sure it'll make us a hell of a lot of money."

"It will," I say with confidence.

His eyes search my face. "I know you said you're taking me out for dinner on Friday, but what about tonight? Do you have plans?"

"I do."

He shifts on the car's seat, so he's facing me directly. I know he wants to ask about my plans, but something is holding him back.

I answer the question I know is sitting on the tip of his tongue. "I'm working at Tin Anchor tonight and tomorrow night. Gage, my boss, asked if I could cover two shifts. I need the extra money, so I couldn't turn it down."

"You make me want to give you a raise." His lips curve into a grin.

"I don't want that," I say quickly. "I wasn't hinting at that. I hope you know that, Sean."

His gaze trails over my face. "I do know that."

"Good." I look out the window to my left before turning back to him. "I'm looking forward to Friday night."

Something has shifted in his expression as he looks deeply into my eyes. "I am too. I'm counting the hours."

CHAPTER THIRTY-THREE

Sean

I STRUCK a nerve with Champ in the car on the way home from work.

My innocent quip about her not-so-subtle way to gain a raise drew a look to her face I hadn't seen before.

Something tells me it has to do with her ex-fiancé.

I couldn't figure anything out about him by sitting at home on my couch, mulling over the very limited clues she's given me about her failed relationship.

That's why I'm back at Harry's place.

It's the distraction I need.

I invited Graham and Kavan to join us for dinner, but Graham tapped out to paint a stencil on the nursery wall.

Kavan is all in, though.

I knock on the door to Harry's townhouse the same way I always do.

This time the response isn't a series of knocks. Instead, the door flies open to reveal Kavan Bane standing behind it.

The man's appearance matches his name.

The ends of his black hair drift over the collar of his suit jacket. His intense blue eyes lock on my face. There's no grin in sight. Instead, he just stares.

"Hey, Bane." I move to embrace him. "It looks like you're in a hell of a good mood tonight."

"I am," he says, tapping the center of my back. "Wedding planning is in full force, Sean."

A few months ago, I would have bet every penny I have on the fact that I'd never hear those words coming out of his mouth.

Kavan hasn't had an easy life. It's gotten much better since he met Juliet Bardin, his fiancée and the woman who has chased away the gray cloud that always hung over his head.

"How's that going for you?" I ask as I inch around him to enter Harry's home.

"I fucking love it."

That turns me right around to face him again.

Kavan isn't one for jokes. I doubt like hell he's ever pulled a prank on anyone, yet this feels surreal. It can't be true.

"You fucking love wedding planning?" I ask to clarify what he just said.

"Yes." The answer is simple and straightforward and accompanied by a broad smile.

"Who the hell are you?" I ask in jest. "The Kavan Bane I know can't smile like that. He's not capable of it."

He wraps one arm around my shoulder to usher me into the hallway that leads to the kitchen. "I'm in love."

I steal a glance at his face. The smile is still planted there.

"Love suits you, Bane."

His hand drifts from my shoulder to pat my cheek. "It's a great feeling, Sean. I'm the luckiest guy in this city."

I could argue that point with him since I feel pretty damn lucky about my upcoming date with Calliope.

The sound of someone descending the staircase pulls my gaze over my shoulder. Dressed in black trousers and a gray sweater, Harrison comes into view.

"Sean." He raises a hand in greeting. "What's on the menu for tonight?"

I didn't bring anything with me because I knew I'd be able to whip up something from what's in Harry's kitchen.

"You name it, I'll cook it," I say.

Harry approaches us. "You've been in an extra good mood lately. What's her name?"

I scratch my jaw, considering the pros and cons of telling these two about the woman I can't stop thinking about.

"It's Callie," Kavan says to Harry. "Calliope Morrow. She's the newest marketing hire at Wells. She lives next door to Sean too."

My head snaps in his direction. "What the fuck?"

Kavan laughs. "Blame Declan. I ran into him the other night at a restaurant opening. Juliet had an invite, so I tagged along."

Of course, my brother would spill the details about Calliope with Kavan.

"This sounds like a double dose of fate, Sean." Harry smiles. "Maybe you'll beat Kavan and Juliet down the aisle."

I chuckle. "Slow down, Harrison. We've been on one date."

"Sometimes, one date is all you need to know." Kavan glances at me. "You should bring her to my wedding, Sean. She can be your plus one."

"When exactly is this wedding happening, Bane?" I ask.

"Three months from today." He glances at Harry before his gaze trails back to me. "I want you to be my best men."

"Best men?" Harry and I ask in unison.

"You two and Locke." Kavan's arms cross his chest. "I make the rules at my wedding, so I'm having three best men."

I trade a look with Harry. The smile on his face says it all. He's in, so I am too. "I'll do my best to be the best man out of the bunch, Bane."

"Good." Kavan turns to Harry. "What about you, Harrison?"

"Count me in." He rests both hands on Kavan's shoulders. "Juliet's been good for you. I've never seen you happier."

Kavan glances at me, but his words are directed to Harry. "Sean looks as happy as me, doesn't he?"

"Almost as happy." Harry waits a moment before he goes on, "I need to say that seeing all of my best friends this happy is good for my heart."

Those words mean a lot coming from him.

"We'll find you someone too," I say as Harry sets off toward the kitchen.

"No need." He shakes his head without glancing back at Kavan or me. "I'm happy with life as it is."

I thought I was too before I met Calliope, but she's brought something into my life that I was missing. I can't put my finger on what that is, but I sure as hell know that I like being around her.

CHAPTER THIRTY-FOUR

Callie

I SPOT Sean the moment he walks into Tin Anchor.

That's a feat in itself, considering the fact that the bar is packed for a Wednesday night. Most of that can be attributed to the two tables of women that arrived an hour ago.

It's obvious that they are celebrating someone's twenty-first birthday.

My co-worker, Angeline, carded everyone in that group. Once that was all straightened away, they ordered a round of shots and a host of other beverages.

Adding to that, several men in suits wandered in, and a quartet of guys in baseball jerseys and jeans.

I keep my gaze trained on Sean as he approaches the bar.

I'm behind it, preparing a mimosa for one of the women at the birthday table.

"Good evening, Champ." Sean's voice sends a shiver straight through me.

I lock eyes with him. "Hey, Saint."

His lips curve into a crooked smile. "This place is hopping tonight. Word must have got out that the most beautiful bartender in the city is on duty."

"Charmer," I quip. "I didn't expect to see you tonight."

His gaze drops to the black T-shirt I'm wearing. It's emblazoned with a small logo that includes the bar's name. "I felt a little parched and thought about tasting your Tom."

Despite my best efforts, a grin tugs at the corner of my lips. "There's an open seat at the end of the bar. I'll start working on your Tom Collins right away."

His gaze darts to the vacant stool a few feet from where he's standing. "I'll be waiting."

I look down at the glass in front of me, but I can sense his eyes are still on me as he makes his way to his seat.

It won't be easy to stay focused on my work knowing he's sitting a few feet away, but I have to do it.

Our combined tip total is already well into the mid-three figures for tonight, and the bar doesn't close for another few hours. Angeline and I will both go home with a tidy sum by the end of the night.

AN HOUR LATER, Sean slides his empty glass toward me. "I was right. Your Tom is better than Rolly's."

My left hand darts to the center of my chest. "I'm touched."

His gaze lingers there, at the spot between my breasts. "I want to touch."

I laugh that off, even though I want that too. I want to feel his hands on every inch of my body.

From the corner of my eye, I spot Angeline approaching where I'm standing. She calls out a drink order that includes another round for the table of women who just sang a rousing yet off-key rendition of *Happy Birthday* to a dark-haired woman in a pink dress.

I repeat the order back to her because that's the only way I'll remember it.

Before I set off to prepare it, I glance at Sean. "Duty calls."

"You don't mind if I hang around until closing time, do you, Champ?"

I was hoping that would happen but certainly didn't expect it. I imagine there are a million things he could be doing other than watching me prepare drinks.

I've only been able to carve out brief moments between orders to talk with him.

"I don't mind that at all." I smile.

"Good." He points at his empty glass. "I'll get another Tom when you have the time. No rush."

Before I can respond, he's sliding a one hundred dollar bill across the bar.

My hand lands on it. "I'll grab your change."

"You'll keep it all." His gaze darts to Angeline. "I'll tip her too before the night is over. I know how brutal it is working a shift like this."

I hold in a laugh. "You don't."

"I do," he insists. "I tended bar in college. It was fucking hard."

"You were a bartender?" I try to mask the surprise in my voice, but I fail miserably.

"I gave it my all." He rubs his jaw. "I got fired during my third shift because I was sampling the product too often."

I nod. "I try to abstain until last call."

"So you'll share a couple of shots with me then?" His

gaze drops to my chest. "After that, I'll take you straight home."

As a blush blooms on my cheeks, I take a step closer to him again and lower my voice. "My home or yours, Saint?"

"Mine." He bites out between clenched teeth. "You're coming home with me tonight."

CHAPTER THIRTY-FIVE

Sean

I WRAP an arm around Calliope's waist to tug her body closer to mine.

The soft sound that escapes her when she feels the length of my erection pressed against her ass is almost enough to make me shoot my load inside my pants.

We're on the subway, headed to our apartment building.

I wanted to call Jurgen, but Champ insisted on this mode of transportation. She told me it would be fun.

I had serious doubts, but I can get on board with her idea of fun if it includes this. We're in a public space, and this feels like it's bordering on foreplay.

Her hand is pressed against mine while she moves her hips in tiny circles as the train races along the track toward our destination.

The few people in this car with us are oblivious to the fact that we're standing when there are many available seats.

I was headed toward one when Calliope curved a finger to lure me closer to her.

"You're making me want to take the subway to work tomorrow," I whisper into the smooth skin of her neck.

Her gaze shoots up so she can lock eyes with me. "I'm game. You never knew it could be this much fun, did you?"

I shake my head. "But you did."

"No." Her voice comes out soft. "I've never done this with anyone else, Sean."

That tightens my grip on her. I want to be her first in every way I can, even if it's something like this with us both fully clothed in a subway car.

"We'll be home soon," she says with another circle of her hips. "I have a challenge for you when we get there."

"Is it whether or not I can keep my mouth off of you in the elevator?" I press my lips to her neck.

A shiver runs through her. "No, but whoever does win the challenge gets to taste the other person first."

I laugh. "There's no way in hell I'm not winning that, Champ. I've wanted a taste of you for so long."

She looks into my eyes again. "I feel the same way about you."

I raise a hand to grab hold of her ponytail so I can tease her head back just a touch more. Then I press my lips to hers for a gentle kiss.

Something tells me after tonight, my life will never be the same again.

I UNLOCK my apartment door but step back to allow Calliope entry first.

Part of that stems from my desire to be a gentleman. A

bigger part of it comes from the fact that I want another look at her ass in the tight jeans she's wearing.

When she left her spot behind the bar earlier to help her co-worker tend to a few tables of patrons, I got my first look at her from head-to-toe.

Everyone else in Tin Anchor did too, and I saw heads turn. Both men and women stared when she walked around the bar in her low-heeled black boots with her ponytail bobbing in the air in an easy rhythm with her steps.

She's effortlessly beautiful. Her body is sensual, even when covered in jeans and a T-shirt.

I wanted her from the first moment I saw her.

Now, I'm mere seconds away from taking her to bed.

Once she's standing in the foyer of my apartment, she spins to face me. "Are you ready for the challenge, Saint?"

I lock the door before I nod. "Bring it on, Champ."

She tugs her black cross-body bag over her shoulder to drop it on a chair in the foyer. "Whoever undresses first gets to taste the other person."

My eyes widen. "If I get my clothes off first, I can eat you out?"

She nods.

"Right here and right now?" I ask for clarification.

Her hands drop to the waistband of her jeans. "When I say three, two, one, go, we do it."

"Let's skip all of that, and I'll drop to my knees now." I take a step closer to her. "You're not going to deny me what I want most in the world, are you?"

Her gaze trails over my suit jacket to my face. "To make it completely fair, you can remove your cufflinks before we start."

I don't know if this game she's playing is making her wet, but I'll take a chance that it is. I want my mouth on her, so I rid myself of my cufflinks, dropping them on the seat of the chair next to her bag. One rolls off and hits the floor with a clink.

She glances at it. "Are those diamond cufflinks?"

I don't know how that matters right now. What matters is that my cock is about to drill a hole through my pants in search of her pussy.

"Yes." My hands hover over the knot of my tie. "Can I lose the tie too?"

Her hands grab hold of the bottom hem of her T-shirt. "You can in three, two, one, go."

I almost strangle myself getting the tie off my neck before buttons scatter to the floor when I rip my shirt apart.

Her eyes are locked on my body as she tugs her T-shirt over her head to reveal a light blue satin bra.

Her nipples are at rapt attention, hard and temping beneath the thin fabric.

Before she's got her jeans unbuttoned, my pants are on the floor.

I kick my shoes off, my socks follow, and with one quick tug of my boxer briefs, I'm done.

Naked and aroused, I stare at her in her bra with her jeans partway down her legs.

"Jesus," I murmur. "You're fucking gorgeous."

Her gaze trails me, stopping to admire my dick. "Sean. You're…"

I drop a hand to fist it, racing my hand over the thick length. "Exactly what you want?"

Without a word, she quickly strips off the rest of her clothes. Her jeans hit the floor, followed by her bra and finally the blue boy shorts she's wearing.

This is the true definition of beauty.

Smooth skin, a mole above her right hipbone, and pink nipples that I can't wait to get my teeth around.

My heart pounds as she whispers something.

"Calliope," I murmur.

"Tell me I won, Sean," she says. "I want to touch you. I want to touch all of you."

Her bare feet pad along the floor as she approaches me. I'm stuck in place, stunned by the sheer beauty I'm witnessing.

She drops to her knees before I can protest, and as I hiss out a breath, she wraps a fist around my dick and licks the crown before it disappears between her plump lips.

My knees quake, but I grab hold of her ponytail, guiding her to take more.

She does until I hit the back of her throat and pure animalistic lust grabs hold of me. Closing my eyes, I pump into her with slow and easy strokes, savoring all of it. "God, you're good. You're so fucking good."

She gifts me with a moan that radiates around the head of my dick.

I lose myself to her then, letting my body take over as she uses her hands, lips, and tongue to take me to the brink.

CHAPTER THIRTY-SIX

Callie

HIS LIPS TRACE a path down my side. He stops to circle his tongue over the mole on my hip. "Calliope."

I don't need to hear more.

I heard everything when he came in the foyer.

The groan that fell from his parted lips was born from somewhere deep inside of him. It was a combination of giving in and the frustration I knew he felt since he'd given up control to me.

But he didn't give it up. I took it.

I wanted him so much. The desire took hold of me like a captor when we were on the subway.

We were fully clothed, but I could feel his erection pressing into me. I could tell he was thick, long, and achingly hard.

All I could think about was getting my mouth on him, so I could watch the accomplished, successful, arrogant businessman come undone under my touch.

I roll onto my back on his bed so I can look into his face.

There's enough light trailing in from the hallway and the floor-to-ceiling window that I can make out every contour of his face and the sharp edge of his trimmed beard.

"You put on a condom," I whisper as his lips press into the soft skin just below my belly button.

"I did, but I want to be bare when I fuck you," he confesses. "I'm clean. I'll get another test if you need that, but I won't press for something that intimate until you're ready."

Something that intimate.

Something that would make me feel so vulnerable.

"The thought of you filled with my cum makes me feel…" His voice trails. "I want to be inside of you."

I shift my body, so my legs part slightly. "I want that."

"You're not ready." His fingers drift from my stomach to my inner thigh. "You're tight. I'll hurt you."

I drop a hand to cover his. I guide him to run his fingertips over my core. "I'm ready, Saint."

His eyes find mine. "You're so fucking wet."

"For you," I manage to whisper the words. "What we did in the foyer. That was hot."

His eyes widen. "You're telling me? I've never come that hard before until now."

"Until now," I echo.

He moves quickly, parting my legs with his body. He settles between them, his eyes never leaving mine. "That was incredible, but coming inside you is going to undo me. I know that."

I look into his eyes. "I'm nervous. I haven't been with anyone in a while."

He pushes a strand of my hair back from my forehead. "I'll be gentle until you beg me not to be."

"I will beg for that," I whisper. "I want it hard. I want to feel you deep."

Before I can say another word, he's lining himself up to my entrance. With a sudden push, he's inside of me. It's a lot, almost too much.

I whimper.

"Calliope." His voice is tender, soothing, and calming in the middle of this storm of need enveloping me. "Easy. We'll go slow."

He plunges forward, each thrust deeper than the last until he's settled inside me.

I look into his face. "Sean."

His response is a circle of his hips before he presses his lips to mine for a lush kiss. "You're beautiful. You're so goddamn beautiful."

Emotion builds inside of me, but I chase it back with a simple plea. "Fuck me."

His lips close around my nipple. The soft touch of his tongue is followed by the sharp bite of his teeth, and each thrust of his body into mine only makes me want more.

I cry out when he shifts to my other nipple, and as he bears down on it, I run my fingers through his hair, tugging on the strands because I want that mouth. I want to feel it on mine.

He gives me that and more as his tongue tangles with mine. I let out short, uneven breaths. His hand drops to my core, and with a flick of his fingertip over my clit, I come hard with a scream from somewhere deep within me.

He fucks me slowly through my release, his finger never leaving the swollen bundle of need. "Again. I want to feel that again."

"I can't," I protest. "I can't."

"You can," he demands before pulling back and flipping me onto my stomach in one easy movement.

Before I can catch my breath, he's inside of me again. The angle is deeper than before, and as I moan from the pleasure mixed with the exquisite bite of pain, he runs his lips over my shoulder.

He fucks me hard, relentlessly, drilling my hips into the softness of his bed until I come again, and he follows with a groan that reverberates through every part of me.

CHAPTER THIRTY-SEVEN

Sean

I STAND behind Calliope and watch her every move.

I had my mouth on her as soon as I tied off the condom and disposed of it in the wastebasket near my bed.

She had already come twice when I was inside her, but I craved more.

I couldn't go another second without tasting her, so I crawled over her and dove between her legs.

I held her against my mouth as she came again for me after I coaxed a finger into her tight channel while I ate her pussy.

I drifted off after that, but obviously, she didn't.

She's wearing her bra and boy shorts. Her T-shirt is still where she dropped it in the foyer, but her jeans have been tossed onto my couch.

She's in front of it, perched on her knees next to my coffee table.

Spread out before her is a bunch of cash.

It's all sorted into piles.

To the side, separate from the rest, are three twenty dollar bills and a ten.

Confused, I whisper her name, hoping I won't scare the hell out of her. "Calliope?"

Panic blankets her expression when she glances over her shoulder at me. She jumps to her feet, spinning to face me. "I thought you were asleep."

I drop a hand to the waistband of my boxer briefs. "I was, but I woke up. I thought you bailed on me."

She mistakes that confession for a suggestion. "I should bail. I mean, I should go home. It's getting late."

I step closer to where she is. "What are you doing?"

Her gaze volleys between the money and me. "I was… those are my tips from tonight."

I look at the money again but don't say a thing.

She scoops up the seventy dollars that she had separated from the rest. She quickly rounds the couch until she's less than a foot from where I'm standing.

My gaze trails over her body. Her skin is flushed, and her hair is a mess. She looks freshly fucked, which only makes me want her more.

Her hand darts out toward me. "I can't keep that tip, Sean. It was too generous. I'll keep thirty if that's okay. Here's the rest."

I stare at the offering in her open palm. "Keep it."

Her hand shakes. "No. I can't. It's too much. It's more than you tipped Rolly."

Rolly isn't a vision of beauty. I'm not falling for him.

"Keep it," I repeat.

"Please." Her voice quakes. "I need you to take this."

Clearly, this isn't about the size of the tip. There's something else going on here, but I don't know whether this is the time to push.

I don't want to taint what we just did with a disagreement about how generous I should be when it comes to her, so I revert to what always works for me when I'm staring down the barrel of an uncomfortable conversation with someone I care about.

Compromise has never let me down yet.

"I'll take it if I can make up the difference in orgasms."

She flashes a wicked smile. "I like the sound of that."

"I'll like the sounds you make when I'm doing that." I chuckle. "Count up your earnings and meet me back in bed. I'll be the guy waiting for you to sit on his face."

"Again?" she asks as she places the money in my hand.

"Again and again, Champ." I slick my tongue over my bottom lip. "The going rate is one dollar for every orgasm. I owe you seventy of them, so let's get to it."

Her eyes widen. "Seventy?"

"Spread over the next week or two."

She moves closer to plant a kiss in the middle of my chest. "Thank you."

I scoop her chin in my hand to lure her gaze up to meet mine. "I haven't paid the difference back yet. You can thank me after I've done that."

"I will," she whispers. "I meant thank you for not asking about all that."

It's taking all the self-control I possess not to ask her why she can't accept the full tip, but I sense she doesn't need me to push her right now.

I glance over her shoulder to the coffee table. "Are you working two jobs right now to save up for something in particular?"

"I am." She bites the corner of her bottom lip. "Freedom."

"Freedom," I repeat the word, not knowing the context but wishing I could give it to her now.

"I'll meet you in the bedroom." Her voice turns playful again. "This has been an incredible night."

"It's not over yet," I remind her with a kiss on her lips before I turn and head back to my bedroom, wishing I could give her everything she needs and more.

CHAPTER THIRTY-EIGHT

CALLIE

I MAKE it to the curb just as Jurgen steers the SUV into a spot next to it.

I snuck out of Sean's apartment shortly after six this morning. I took a long, hot shower, ate a bowl of cereal for breakfast, and then got ready for the day.

I needed the time to find my bearings again after last night.

I've had lovers in the past, but not one of them made me feel all the things I felt when I was in bed with Sean. I felt beautiful and cherished, but mostly I felt alive.

My life has been buried under a mountain of worry for so long that I forgot how it feels to let go and enjoy myself.

That doesn't mean I can lose sight of my goals, but it does mean that I have something to look forward to. Spending time with Sean is just what I need right now, and I hope it doesn't end anytime soon.

"Champ!" Sean calls my nickname from somewhere to my right.

I glance over to see him wearing a dark gray suit, a light blue button-down shirt, and a striped blue tie. He's leaning a shoulder against the glass façade of the building next door.

"Hey," I say as I wait for him to join me.

He pushes away from the building to take a few measured steps toward me. "You look lovely today, Calliope."

I look down at the black skirt and pink blouse I'm wearing. Both were recent finds at the vintage store that I love. The blouse still had the original tag when I purchased it for less than five dollars.

"You look great too for someone who barely slept."

He steps closer to lean toward me. His voice lowers. "If having you in my bed means little sleep for me, I can live with that."

I glance up and into his eyes. Words escape me, so I offer him a soft smile.

He gestures past me toward the street. "Time to hit the road."

I turn to approach the waiting car. "Good morning, Jurgen."

"Good morning, Callie," he greets me the way he always does. "You're looking well this early a.m., Mr. Wells."

"I'm feeling better than I have in a hell of a long time, Jurgen."

After what we did last night, hearing those words from Sean warms me from the inside out.

I settle onto the back seat of the car. Sean does the same, but he glides closer to me than he ever has before.

When I look into his face, a smile is playing on his lips.

"What?" I ask playfully. "You look like you have a secret."

"I've figured out a secret," he says. "It's the secret to happiness."

Expecting him to tell me that it has something to do with sex, I ask the obvious question. "What's the secret to happiness?"

His gaze trails over my face. "I'm looking at her."

For the first time in what feels like forever, hope blooms inside of me. Maybe, just maybe, there is a chance for me to be happy too.

DELORA COMES CHARGING toward where I'm sitting at a conference table with Justin and Rory. We've been buoying ideas around about the potential new ad campaign.

Not only did Delora assign all of us the task of getting everything in order for the presentation she'll be making to Sean and Declan, but she also wants us to craft a list of innovative ways to market the subscription model.

She had already jotted down online marketing and a new billboard in Times Square, but she suggested that we think outside the traditional box, so that's what all three of us have been focused on this morning.

"Hey, Delora." Justin waves at her as she steps into the conference room. "You're running late today."

The broad smile that slides over her mouth says it all. She has good news.

"Delora?" Rory questions her as he rakes a hand through his short blond hair. "What's up?"

Excitement grips her from the inside out because she bounces in place. She literally bobs up and down in her heels. "I'm getting married!"

All three of us are on our feet in a flash. I race around the conference table, but Justin and Rory beat me to our boss.

They both gather her in an embrace, and as I round the table, their hands wave in my direction.

Growing up in a family with four kids, I know that signal. It's the universal sign for '*get-in-on-this-hug.*' Justin and Rory step apart to give me room, so I wrap my arms around Delora to offer her my congratulations.

"I'm so fucking excited!" she exclaims. "Did you all see the ring?"

We part so we can each take a turn admiring the emerald and diamond ring on her finger.

"It's gorgeous," I murmur. "It's beautiful, Delora."

"We couldn't afford an engagement ring for our first wedding," she says with tears streaming down her cheeks. "Larry told me that he wanted to do it right this time. When he dropped to his knee last night and flashed this beauty at me, how the hell could I say no to that?"

"You couldn't." Justin steals a look at Rory. "I couldn't say no when my man asked me to marry him either."

My head snaps to the left. That's when I see a sight that brings tears to my eyes.

With an arm wrapped around Rory's shoulder, Justin holds up his left hand to show off a gorgeous black band marked with two red stones.

Rory's left hand pops up, and sitting on his ring finger is an identical ring.

"Are you two married?" Delora asks with her mouth falling open. "When the hell did that happen?"

"Engaged," Justin corrects her. " It happened a few days ago. We were waiting for the right time to tell you."

"I'm so happy for both of you," I say before Delora repeats the same phrase.

Justin beams. "The wedding will be next summer in the South of France. Everyone in this room is invited, of course."

Rory pokes an elbow into my side. "That just leaves you, Callie. You're the only holdout. You need to find a man worthy of you so we can celebrate your wedding too."

I glance down at my bare finger.

I once thought I'd be happily married by now, but I'm more grateful than I've ever been that I walked away from that relationship.

"Don't rush her." Delora swats a hand over Rory's shoulder. "When it's meant to be, it'll happen. Right, Callie?"

"Right." I agree with a brisk nod of my chin.

"Let's get to work." Delora heads toward the conference table. "We're going to do everything in our power to impress the Wells brothers so I can jet off to my honeymoon without a care in the world."

CHAPTER THIRTY-NINE

Sean

MY PLAN for tonight was a repeat of last night, but Declan tossed a wrench into the middle of that.

I was prepared to go to Tin Anchor this evening, sip on a drink crafted by the hand of the most beautiful bartender in Manhattan, and then spend the remainder of my night in bed with her.

My brother decided that this would be the perfect night for the two of us to head over to our parents' Manhattan residence to start cleaning out a storage room that we've neglected for a hell of a long time.

Since their home on the Upper West Side is about to undergo a slew of renovations, the clock was ticking.

We have until the end of the month to get what we want out of the storage room, or in the eloquent words of our mother, "the lot of it will be burned and trashed."

Considering that many of the cardboard boxes in there

contain mementos from when we were kids, you'd think that our mom would view them as having some sentimental value.

She doesn't.

I round the corner toward the townhouse that I grew up in.

I remember racing up and down this sidewalk chasing my older brother while he held his cherished baseball glove just out of my reach.

I fondly recall helping Ava find her balance in a pair of roller skates she got for her tenth birthday.

I have little to complain about in terms of my childhood. I was fortunate in that I've always had parents who loved me. My father's support throughout school and college came when I needed it the most.

I'd left the cocoon of a world where I was viewed as a great guy. I did whatever it took to make the people around me happy. If that meant sitting up all night to study because my sister had a test and no belief in her ability to pass it, I was by her side.

I passed on outings with my friends and invitations to weekend getaways to Westhampton with relatives when one of my parents needed a hand.

I was their saint. That's what they all called me because I was always the one who would drop everything in his life to make someone else's better.

I'll still do that, but with the knowledge that people think a saint can do no wrong. I can do wrong, and I have.

I was busted by my mom for being drunk when I was fourteen, and I got pulled over for speeding on my drive up to The Buchanan School after a weekend in the city when I was seventeen.

The police officer found a small zip-top bag in my pocket. I had smoked the weed that had been in it days before, but the scent still lingered. He detained me and reached out to my parents to fill them in on what had happened.

My mother swore I'd tarnished the family name. My dad told me to double-check all of my pockets before I set out on the open road again.

Neither of those things compared to my transgression when I was days short of my eighteenth birthday. I'd taken one of my senior classmates to the ground with a punch to his face. I did that after I caught him bullying a freshman that couldn't defend himself. I got in the middle of it because I had to. It was that simple to me.

It earned me a month-long suspension from The Buchanan School, and I was banned from graduation ceremonies. All of that was the result of my being arrested for the punch. The charges were dropped, but I felt the impact of that night for a long time afterward, mainly because I'd let my dad down.

"Saint!"

I glance over my shoulder when I hear that name and the familiar voice attached to it.

Declan, dressed in jeans and a black sweatshirt, smiles at me as he jogs along the sidewalk with a white paper bag in his hand.

It's rare for me to see my brother like this without the power suits and styled hair.

He looks like the fifteen-year-old kid who got a tattoo on his chest by flashing a fake ID at a tattoo shop on the Lower East Side.

I give him a once over. "That's a look, Decky."

Coming to a stop beside me, he runs his hands over the front of the shirt. "I've already been here for an hour. I found this in the storage room. What do you think?"

I tug on the hood. "I think it's too fucking tight. Can you breathe?"

"Barely." He huffs out a laugh. "I ran out to grab us some dinner."

I glance at the bag. "What did you get?"

"Chili fries and loaded hot dogs." He grins. "Remember when we'd sneak this into my room? Mom was never the wiser."

Happy to burst his bubble of oblivion, I pat his shoulder. "She always knew. Dad would keep her at bay by dancing with her."

Both of his brows pop up. "You're serious?"

"Dead serious." I smile. "Since they're in Florida, we can enjoy our dinner on mom's best dishes and crack open a bottle of granddad's scotch."

He shakes his head. "We'll be in supreme shit if we do that."

"I'm not going to tell." I start walking toward our parents' home. "Are you?"

"No way in hell," he says from behind me. "But let's leave granddad's scotch alone. There are only three bottles left. He wanted each of us to open one on our wedding days."

I wait for him to catch up, so we're walking side-by-side. "Why wait for that? Ava can never get married because no man on this earth is good enough for her. Besides, you're a confirmed bachelor for life, right?"

"You never know what tomorrow brings, Sean." He inches ahead of me. "I'll race you to the door. First one there has to carry the heavy boxes out."

He takes off in a sprint.

I watch him from behind, feeling damn lucky that I'm his little brother.

CHAPTER FORTY

Callie

I HEAVE a sigh of relief as I step into the cool night air. My shift at Tin Anchor tonight was busier than usual, but it was definitely worth my while.

I walked out of there with more than seven hundred dollars in tips. With shaking hands and tears of joy welling in my eyes, I shoved it, along with my tips from last night, into one of the plain white envelopes that Gage keeps in his office.

I just dropped that envelope into the hand of a trusted friend.

I glance over my shoulder one last time to see him tucking it into his pocket.

"Calliope?" That voice, with its deep melodic tones and toe-curling rasp, is as unique as the man it belongs to.

I turn to my right to see Sean approaching me.

Panic shoots through me.

I don't want him to see me here. He can't see me here.

This is a part of the world that I ran from.

"Hi," I whisper, unsure of what to say.

I assumed he'd eventually show up at Tin Anchor tonight after spending some time at home, but he's still wearing the same suit and shirt he had on at work.

Maybe he had dinner plans or more-than-dinner plans with another woman.

His mussed hair and the end of his tie peeking out from one pocket of his suit jacket suggest that Sean had a lot of fun with someone tonight.

My gaze drifts to something tucked under his arm.

I can't quite make out what it is.

He glances at the glass doors that lead into the lobby of the building I just exited. "What are you doing in this neighborhood?"

"I got off work a bit ago," I offer while I struggle to find the words to explain why I'm so far from home at this time of night.

He rakes me from head to toe, taking in my outfit. It's the same jeans and Tin Anchor T-shirt that I wore last night. I washed them early this morning, tossed them in the dryer as I ate a quick dinner, and then took off for work.

I tuck a strand of my hair behind my ear. "What are you doing in this neighborhood?"

I sense that my non-explanation of what I'm doing here doesn't please him, but he answers my question. "Decky and I were at our parents' home. It's a couple of blocks from here. We have to clear out some stuff."

"Stuff like that?" I point at whatever is under his arm.

He yanks it out. It's a well-worn leather baseball glove. "Lots of stuff like this. Stuff from when we were kids. This is Declan's old baseball glove. When I was nine, I wanted this more than anything. I finally got it in my hands tonight."

He's so open and honest.

It pains me that I can't be that way with him.

My gaze shoots to the left when one of the doors to the building opens, and the doorman peeks his head out. He looks at Sean before turning his attention to me. "I wanted to thank you again for the pen, Miss Morrow. I know you said you'd take the subway home, but I can call for a car if that's preferable. It is getting quite late."

Sean shoves a hand at him. "How are you? I'm Sean."

"I'm Leon."

Wishing Leon would go back to his post inside, I smile. "I don't need a car. I'll be fine."

Sean drops Leon's hand after a hearty shake. "I can attest to that. I'll see Calliope home."

Leon's gaze lingers on my face. "Very well. It was good to see you again, Miss Morrow. If I didn't mention it earlier, I miss you."

"I miss you too," I whisper. "Please take care."

He offers Sean a nod before he retreats back inside the building.

Sean glances at me. "I needed some fresh air, so I planned to walk a few blocks before calling Jurgen to pick me up. I'll call him now and get him to head in our direction."

"There's a subway stop at the end of the block. Are you game to take another ride with me?"

He holds out his hand. "I'd never say no to that."

We set off in that direction holding hands. As we near the corner, Sean tugs on my hand to slow my pace. He turns to look down at me. "Are you and Leon old friends?"

"We are," I answer honestly, feeling brave enough to make a small confession because he deserves that. "I used to live there."

"Did you live there recently?"

I can't be surprised that he wants to know more, so I nod. "Until six months ago. Then I moved to a one bedroom apartment that I shared with a few friends from college."

His left brow perks. "You left?"

I know he's looking for more than a simple answer to that question, so I step closer to him. I reach up to touch his jaw with my fingers. "I left. I didn't belong there."

"I understand," he murmurs. "So you stopped by to drop off a pen for Leon?"

The next words that will come out of my mouth aren't an outright lie, but they will omit something that I'm not ready to share with him yet. "Sometimes people leave pens on the bar if they write their phone numbers on cocktail napkins. Leon collects silver pens, so whenever I see one that's abandoned, I save it for him."

"You mean sometimes men leave their pens on the bar when they write down their numbers for you?"

I laugh. "Yes, but I almost always toss those in the trash."

"Almost always?" He rubs his jaw. "Did you keep any of those numbers tonight?"

"Why would I?" I step closer to him. "Have you seen my neighbor? You won't believe what he can do with his mouth and hands. Not to mention what's inside his boxer briefs."

He skims a hand down the front of his shirt. "If you think he's all that, he's one lucky bastard."

"I'm one very lucky woman."

"You're an incredible woman." He gazes into my eyes. "You have a good heart, Champ. Leon and I can both attest to that."

I'm grateful that he didn't push me on why I didn't wait until tomorrow to bring Leon his pen. I couldn't wait because I want that envelope in my ex-fiancé's hand as soon as possible.

"I'll walk you home now," he says.

"You'll take the subway home with me now."

His lips press into mine again for another kiss. "I'd like to repay some of that seventy dollars worth of orgasms I owe you tonight."

Laughing, I tug on his hand to get him moving. "I can't wait."

CHAPTER FORTY-ONE

Sean

THE DESIRE TO go back to the building where Leon works so I can pound on every door until I find Calliope's ex is strong, but I'm not that guy.

I might have been if we hadn't fallen into my bed an hour ago.

After what we just shared, I don't need to know the name of the bastard she was engaged to. I don't have to see his face. She wants me now, and that's all that matters.

I must be doing something right if this woman next to me in my bed thinks I'm worth her time.

She slides her bare leg over mine. "You're an amazing lover."

I've heard those words in the past but their gravity, the weight in which they were spoken, never resonated with me. Tonight I feel them.

"Being with you is an out-of-body experience, Calliope."

I tug her closer to me so I can rest my chin on the top of her head. "It's hard to describe."

She pulls back to glance up, so our eyes meet. "I understand because I feel the same way."

I think this might be love, and if it is, I'm falling hard and fast for her.

"You had this look in your eyes when I first saw you tonight." I tread into a topic I swore I wouldn't with her, but things have shifted. She's no longer as hesitant as when we first agreed to see each other.

"This look?" she asks as she widens her eyes. "It's my *damn-my-boss-is-hot –as-fuck* look."

I huff out a laugh. "You think I'm hot as fuck?"

"You know you are." She sighs. "That's why you put yourself on that billboard in Times Square."

"Did you figure that out on your own, or did you have Delora's help?"

"Delora," she admits. "But I get why you did it. You have quite a body to work with."

My hand slides down her back. "As do you, Champ."

She squirms against me. "Tell me more about this look I had tonight."

"It's the look a woman has when she spots that one face out of all the millions of faces in Manhattan. It's the face of the guy she knows is crazy about her."

Her cheeks blush pink as her gaze drops to my lips. "You're crazy about me?"

I skim my fingertips over her back until I reach the base of her neck. "So fucking crazy about you."

She kisses me in a way that makes every fear I've ever had disappear.

I cling to her, savoring the taste of her lips, cherishing

each of her breaths, and wishing I had met her years before now.

As we part, she stares into my eyes. "Make love to me, Sean."

Nothing leaves my lips but a low groan of desire.

I roll her onto her back and stare down at her beautiful face.

I sense that unspoken words are sitting on her tongue, but I get it. I get that the idiot that lives in that building on the Upper West Side broke her in a sense, and she's piecing herself back together in the way she needs to.

I kiss her mouth before I trail my lips down her chest until they settle over her right nipple. I know her body. I know that my mouth on that sweet swollen bud will draw her hips up.

I know that when I lick up the seam between her legs, she'll shudder before she quietly begs me to suck on her clit.

I lower myself, tasting a path down her body until my face is between her thighs. "This first. Then I want to be inside of you."

"Don't be gentle tonight," she whispers, fingers threading through my hair. "I want to feel you everywhere."

I attack her core with relish, licking, nipping, sucking, biting, and finally sliding a finger into her tight channel.

She bucks against me, chanting my name in a hymn that will lull me to sleep when she leaves me tonight.

"OUR DATE IS TONIGHT," Calliope reminds me as we wait on the sidewalk for Jurgen to arrive.

She left me early this morning again to get ready for the day.

By the time my alarm rang, she was gone, so I got up, showered, had a coffee, and forged a plan for the day.

It'll be a busy one, but the reward of having dinner with her will be the end goal I'll focus on.

I give her a once over, admiring the cut of the emerald green dress she's wearing. On her feet are black heels with little bows at the back of the ankle.

In addition to looking completely professional, she's sexy as hell.

That's not an easy combination to pull off, but she does it each and every day.

"Should I lose the suit after work?" I smooth a palm over one of the lapels of my dark blue suit jacket. "Are we dining at a formal or casual place?"

Her gaze slides over me, taking time to admire everything. "Casual."

"So, no suit?"

"Depends on how you define casual." She looks down at her dress. "I'm wearing this."

"That's not casual," I point out while glancing at the approaching traffic to see if I spot Jurgen. "Those tight ripped jeans you wear are casual. Those T-shirts that cling to your body are casual."

She takes a step forward while giving her hips a wiggle. "This clings."

"Damn right it does."

A smile blooms on her mouth. "Wear whatever feels comfortable for you. I'll keep this on because it's a special dress. I wear it on special occasions."

"This is sounding less casual by the second, Champ."

With a mischievous grin, she shrugs. "It's casual. I consider my treating you to dinner as a special occasion. I promise you'll have a good time."

The black SUV pulling in next to the curb is all too familiar. I raise a hand in greeting to my driver. "Every moment I'm fortunate enough to spend with you is a good time. I'm really looking forward to tonight, Calliope."

"I am too," she says. "I think it will be a night to remember."

CHAPTER FORTY-TWO

CALLIE

"ISN'T THIS TYPICALLY A TUESDAY THING?" Sean tosses me a smile as I stand in line, waiting to order our dinner.

We're near Radio City Music Hall. It's almost seven p.m., and the sun's warmth is starting to give way to a gentle breeze.

I checked the forecast before we left the office to make sure I didn't have to borrow an umbrella from the holder that sits behind the reception desk in the lobby.

Sean's last call of the day ran late, so while I waited for him, I jotted down more marketing ideas for the subscription model. I'm excited to run them by Rory and Justin on Monday morning before we present all of our ideas to Delora.

"Not in my world," I quip. "It's a whenever the craving strikes thing. What do you want me to get for you?"

His gaze wanders to the simple menu on the front of the food truck. "You choose."

"You're sure?"

"I trust you, Champ." He moves so he's standing next to me. "I'm on board for whatever you're eating."

Nodding, I take a step forward until I'm at the window. "Hey, Barney!"

The owner of the food truck shoots me a broad smile. "Callie Morrow! Look at you. Let me guess. An order of fish tacos, chips and salsa on the side, and a bottle of water."

"Times two." I hold out some cash.

Barney's gaze wanders to Sean. "Boyfriend?"

"I am," Sean says before I can introduce him as my boss or my neighbor. "Sean Wells."

"I'm pleased to meet you." Barney straightens the apron tied around his waist. "Be good to her. She deserves only the best."

Sean's gaze catches mine. "I agree. Calliope deserves only the best."

AN HOUR LATER, we walk into a gallery a few blocks from where we sat to eat our dinner.

Sean complimented the food and told me he planned on stopping by the truck for lunch one day with his brother in tow.

I took that to mean that I'd made a wise decision taking him there.

As we enter the small space, Sean takes a look around. "Another hidden gem. I didn't know this place existed, Champ."

There are treasures like this sprinkled throughout Manhattan.

I've been fortunate because at one time, I'd spend hours

walking the streets of this city with my camera in my hand. It was the ideal way to clear my mind after a long day of college classes. Once I graduated, I'd spend time each weekend strolling along a street I'd never been on before.

I snapped thousands of images. Each was unique in that it captured a specific moment in time in this city.

Life changed, so that passion fell by the wayside, but coming to exhibit openings like this reminds me that creativity exists all around us, even if we can't actively pursue it at the moment.

"I found this place about a year ago," I tell him as I look around the space.

This month's exhibit features a sculptor from Brooklyn. His medium is clay, and the sculptures are all of animals, each measuring no more than six inches in height and a foot across.

"The owner only works with up-and-coming artists," I explain to Sean. "She chooses someone who she feels has potential. They are given one area of the gallery to showcase their work. It's priced at what they view as fair, and she takes a very small percentage. It's up to the artist to cover the cost of the opening of their exhibit."

His gaze travels over the small stands that hold the sculptures beneath glass covers. From our vantage point I spot a horse, a lion with an impressive mane, and the head of a dog with tipped ears.

"My favorite is the deer." A woman moves to stand next to us. "We spotted it when we were on a camping trip upstate last year."

I turn to her. "You're the sculptor?"

She lets out a surprised laugh. "No. I'm afraid I don't have an artistic bone in my body. My son created all of these."

"He's very talented." I glance at all the people milling about checking out the sculptures. "All of the pieces are so detailed. They're breathtaking."

Her gaze volleys between Sean's face and mine. "Thank you for coming. Adam is stunned at the turnout."

I look over to see a young man standing away from the crowd. "Is that Adam?"

"He's fifteen," she explains. "This exhibit is the start of big things for him. I think he's overwhelmed at the moment. I told him it's only a matter of time until he sells out."

"I think you're right." Sean smiles at her. "I think this is the beginning of great things for your son."

CHAPTER FORTY-THREE

Sean

"I WOULD HAVE BOUGHT one of Adam's sculptures if they didn't all get scooped at record speed," I confess to Calliope as we step out of the gallery.

She laughs. "You would have?"

"Damn right." I tug her hand into mine. "What's better than funding someone's dreams?"

"You really are a saint."

"I'm also a sinner, but you know that." I wiggle my brows.

"I do know that." Chuckling, she motions to the right. "Our next stop is this way."

"My bed is this way." I point to the left. "I think we should stop there for the night or the weekend if you're up to it."

"I can't stay all weekend." She sighs. "I'm working a double shift at Tin Anchor tomorrow, and on Sunday, I'm going to Delora's apartment with Justin and Rory. We'll go over everything before Delora makes the presentation on Monday."

I know I can't crash the meeting at Delora's apartment, so I set out a compromise. "Spend the morning with me. I'll cook you breakfast."

"You make a great dinner. I can't begin to imagine what you'll prepare for breakfast."

I drop a glance at my watch. "You're just twelve hours away from finding out."

She tugs on my hand to get me moving. "We're just three blocks away from our next stop on this date."

I see the theme of this date night even if she doesn't want me to.

The tacos were a steal of a deal. The exhibit opening at the gallery was free for all. We've journeyed around midtown Manhattan on foot since riding the subway here after work.

Champ is giving me the date of my dreams on a budget that works for her.

I damn well wish I could give her a raise, but I sense that would cause more harm than good for our developing relationship.

As we approach the corner on the crowded sidewalk, I squeeze her hand. "How do you feel about what I said earlier, Calliope?"

Her gaze jumps to my face. "What did you say earlier?"

I'll repeat it twenty times if she needs me to because I like the sound of it that much. "I introduced myself to Barney as your boyfriend."

That stops her in place. She turns, so she's facing me directly. "Are you my boyfriend?"

I drop to a knee because I want her to remember this date as fondly as I will.

Her mouth drops open, so I speed this up because I may be crazy about her, but I'm not proposing marriage.

"Will you do me the honor of being my girlfriend, Champ?"

"Yes," she says as people around us call out congratulations based on their assumptions of what they think they are witnessing. "I'd love to be your girlfriend."

I FOLLOW Calliope into the lobby of our building.

It's almost midnight.

Our date night trek around midtown Manhattan ended less than thirty minutes ago.

After we stopped at a wine bar owned by one of Champ's former co-workers, we took in the sights, sounds, and scents of Times Square. I can't recall the last time I was down there, but tonight left me with a great memory of the area.

As we strolled hand-in-hand through the raucous Friday night crowds, Calliope broke free and took off in a sprint.

I followed fast on her heel and broke out laughing when I saw where she was headed.

She had spotted someone dressed in a Smurf costume, so she posed next to them while I snapped a few pictures on my phone. I put some money in their palm and thanked the mysterious stranger for capping off a memorable night.

"You'll note that there are absolutely no palm prints on my dress," she calls over her shoulder to me. "That Smurf is all gentleman, all the time."

That's interesting, considering the person who thanked me for tipping them for their time had a female voice.

"Lucky for him," I quip.

She slows slightly as her phone starts ringing.

Before she digs her hand into her purse to fish for it, her gaze jumps to my face. "Calls at this time of night are never good."

They are par for the course in my world. Our products are stocked in stores worldwide, and we have branch offices in many countries. It's not unusual for me to get a call at this time or later if a problem pops up.

"You should answer," I suggest even though she's staring into her bag in search of her phone.

Her gaze jumps to the screen as soon as she's got the phone in her hand.

She taps her thumb on it to decline the call. "It's no one."

The evident frustration lacing those three words suggests that it's someone she doesn't want to talk to.

"Who was it?" I ask.

Jealousy is a beast I have no experience battling, but I feel it brewing inside of me now.

Her non-answer pushes me into a place I don't want to go, but curiosity is driving me. "Was it your ex, Calliope?"

She jabs a finger into the elevator call button more than once. "It's no one, Sean."

I move to stand next to her. "Do you still speak with him?"

She lets out an audible sigh. "There are some loose ends that I'm trying to tie up with him. That's all that call was about."

"Loose ends late on a Friday night?"

Jesus, I sound like a bastard.

Judging by the look on her face, she sees me in the same light. "I declined the call because I don't want to talk to him tonight."

That should satisfy me, but I see how her hands are shaking. I can hear the sound of her labored breaths. Whatever went down between her and this guy gutted her.

We step into the elevator car in silence.

I push the button for our floor and then realize her gaze is on me.

I turn to face her. "I'm here if you ever need to talk about anything, Calliope. I once told you that I'm a good friend. I mean it."

Her hand moves to tug on the bottom of my tie. "Thank you, Sean."

"I should be the one thanking you for a great night," I say to lighten the mood. "This was the best date I've ever been on."

She wraps her fist around the tie to yank me closer. "I doubt that."

I reach to slide a fingertip over her chin. "Don't doubt anything I say to you. Our date was one for the record books. I'll never forget this night."

As the doors slide open on our floor, she glances in that direction. "I won't either. I think I'm going to turn in. You've worn me out the past few nights, and I want to be rested for my shift tomorrow."

I don't want the date to end this way, so I offer a compromise. "If you come home with me, I promise I'll tuck you in next to me and let you sleep."

She steps out of the elevator with me right behind her.

As she nears her apartment door, she slows to a stop.

I can tell she's hesitating, so I up my offer to what I promised her earlier before her ex called and splintered this date. "I'll cook you breakfast in the morning, and that will leave you plenty of time to get ready for your shift."

Her gaze snakes up my body until our eyes are locked. "I'd like that."

I'd like more, but if she needs me to hold her while she sleeps and cook for her before she heads to her second job, I'll shine at both.

"You're a pretty great boyfriend."

"I'm the best boyfriend," I say, wanting that to be true.

I want to be the man of her dreams. I want to right every wrong that's been done to her. I want the guy who just called to be such a distant memory to her that she can't recall anything about him.

I unlock the door to my apartment and swing it open. "After you, Champ. Tonight I take care of you."

CHAPTER FORTY-FOUR

CALLIE

I STARE into his deep brown eyes as we lie beside each other in his bed. Daybreak is upon us. The light filtering into the window is soothing and soft, showcasing the sharp cut of his jaw beneath his beard.

"You have a good soul," I whisper to him.

Sean's lips curve up in an almost grin. "Do I?"

I study his face with the faint lines that trail out from the corners of his eyes and the tiny scar that sits just below his left eyebrow. He's strikingly handsome, yet something about him hints at vulnerability beneath the surface.

"You told me that you were nicknamed Saint because you've always helped out anyone who needed it."

His eyes drop to my lips. "I do what anyone would do."

I shake my head slightly, my cheek sinking into the pillow my head is resting on. "You go above and beyond."

"How so?"

I can't tell if the question is serious or not, so I point out an example. "You spend time with our neighbors because they miss their grandchildren."

"I miss my grandparents," he admits. "It's kind of a win-win for all of us."

"You tip really well."

He lets out a low chuckle that shakes his bare chest. "I can afford to, and every person I tip well deserves it."

"What's the kindest thing you've ever done for someone, Sean?" I ask, hoping he won't toss out a joke or try to divert with humor.

"Kindness is in the eye of the beholder," he counters.

"In the eyes of this beholder, you're very kind." I smile.

His left hand jumps to cradle my cheek. "I'd do anything for you, Calliope. If you had something you needed help with, I'd do what I could without any questions."

"I know," I whisper.

"I don't need to know everything about your past." His fingers press into my cheek. "But if there is any way that I can ease a burden that you're carrying, I want to do that for you."

I slide forward so I can press my entire nude body against his.

He promised to let me sleep last night, but I wanted more. Once I was settled in bed next to him, I couldn't resist kissing him. That quickly progressed into touching each other, and a fuck that left me feeling boneless.

I run my fingertips over the carved muscles of his shoulder. "I have to carry my burden alone."

He bites his bottom lip. "That kills me, Champ. It's hard not to help you."

I know if I asked him to help me, I'd be free of my ex today. Sean would take care of it. He'd rid me of that burden, but then I'd be indebted to him, and I can't put myself in that position again with another wealthy man.

He wraps both arms around me, tugging me even closer. "Before I make breakfast for you, let me show you how much you mean to me."

I bite back tears because I never knew I could feel like this with a man. I feel safe and treasured. Sean makes me feel content in a way I never have before.

"How can I turn that down?"

"You can't." He laughs. "I still owe you a fuck ton of orgasms, so let's get to it. Tell me how you want it. I'm here to please you."

I push on his broad shoulders until he's flat on his back. I slide down the sheet shielding his groin before he can say anything.

Wrapping my hands around his thick length, I bow my head. "I want this."

His hand falls into my hair. His fingers weave between the strands. "I want you to want it."

"You're welcome," I whisper as I look at his face.

A bark of laughter falls from his lips. "I didn't say thank you."

I lick a slow path over the crown of his cock. "You will."

―――――

TWO HOURS LATER, Sean adjusts the front of my dress before he holds out my shoes. "Do you want me to help you put these on, or will you head home barefoot?"

I take the heels from him. "Barefoot."

He tugs on the waistband of the gray sweatpants he's wearing. He pulled on those before heading out of the bedroom to make breakfast.

The spread was impressive. Everything from perfectly cooked bacon to scrambled eggs and a platter of fresh fruit greeted me when I made it to the dining room table wearing only my bra and panties.

"Thank you again for everything," I whisper. "I had an incredible night and morning."

"Me too," he murmurs. "I'd follow you to work today, but Decky and I are meeting at the office late this afternoon to go over a few things."

"Work on a Saturday?" I question. "I would have thought the boss could get away with taking the weekends off."

"My brother's guilt-wielding powers are second to none." He chuckles. "We have a few things that need our attention, so we'll do that today."

Feeling disappointed that I won't see him at the bar, I sigh. "I should get going. I need to shower, and I promised my sister I'd call her this morning."

He perks a brow.

"She loves to talk on the phone." I draw out the words. "I usually put it on speaker and go about doing what I need to do."

He runs a hand along my cheek. "Maybe one day soon I can meet your sister."

"Naomi would love that." I take a breath. "She had a few things to say about that billboard in Times Square."

"All good things," he says, but it doesn't sound the least bit arrogant.

I pat the center of his bare chest. "All great things. You know that the billboard is the highlight of many people's visits to Times Square."

His hand reaches to cup mine so I can feel the steady beating of his heart. "I know that when we passed it yesterday, you snuck a look at it."

"Guilty as charged," I admit. "Now that I know it's you, I can't help but look."

"You can touch all you want, Champ." He guides my hand down his chest toward his stomach. "All of this is yours for the taking whenever you want."

I want it always and forever.

More than that, I want his heart.

I think I'm falling in love with him.

It may be too soon or too fast, but it feels like love, and it's more intense than anything I've felt before.

"Kiss me goodbye." He leans forward. "I want to taste you on my lips until I see you again."

I shoot up to my tiptoes to press my mouth to his.

Our kiss is slow, torturous, and literally weakens my knees. I lean into Sean to find my balance.

"That was…" His voice trails. "Heaven, Calliope."

"Think about me today," I whisper.

"I do. Every single second." He kisses me again. "I can't help it. You're the best thing that's ever happened to me."

CHAPTER FORTY-FIVE

Sean

"TODAY IS THE DAY!" Calliope's smile brightens the overcast streets of Manhattan as soon as she exits our building.

For someone who spent all of her weekend immersed in work, she looks like a million bucks.

Her hair is pinned up in a messy bun. Her body is wrapped in a fitted black dress with lace trim at the hem, and the black heels on her feet give her a few extra inches in height.

She's a dream to look at and incredible to touch.

Since we're on the sidewalk outside our building with people milling about, I resist the urge to pull her in for a kiss.

Instead, I stare. I outright stare at her as she approaches me.

"Hi, Sean," she says as she nears me.

I flash her a smile. "Hey, you."

Her gaze trails over the dark gray suit I'm wearing. "You're a sight for sore eyes."

I step toward her because even though it may not be appropriate for me to kiss her the way I want to right now, I need to be closer to her. "You look phenomenal."

"It's all smoke and mirrors." She twirls, giving me the full three hundred and sixty degree view. "I'm dead tired."

"Yet, you're excited for today," I point out.

"How can I not be?" Her gaze trails from my face to the approaching traffic. "Delora is going to blow you away with her presentation today."

I hope to hell she's right.

Delora needs to impress me, but she has to sell the subscription idea to Declan as well.

I have the authority to give it the green light without his approval, but I won't. I need him to be as much on board as I am.

"You're confident that it'll be a go."

She nods. "I know it'll be a go. We put our all into this."

Seeing her like this makes me want to push the project forward sight unseen.

"Jurgen's coming." Her finger darts in the air, pointing over my shoulder. "I can't wait to get to the office."

"Champ," I say her name to lure her attention back to me. "I'm proud of you."

Her bottom lip quivers before she sinks her top teeth into it to still it. "Sean."

I can tell those words hit her deeply. "You've been working very hard. Let me cook for you tonight."

"I'm cooking for you tomorrow night."

I glance to where Jurgen is parking the SUV next to the curb. "You are?"

"For everyone." Her hand waves toward the entrance to our building. "I ran into Mrs. Sweeney yesterday. I asked if she could come for dinner tomorrow. She said yes, and passed it along to Mrs. Fields and the Durkmans, so I texted Brandi this morning to see if they are free, and they'll be there."

I take that all in as she approaches the open car door.

"I wanted to invite you in person," she says once she's settled on the seat. "You don't have plans, do you?"

If I did, I'd cancel them. "I'll be there."

"Good." She lets out a sigh. "Tonight, Delora is taking Justin, Rory, and me out for dinner to celebrate."

I reach to grab her hand as Jurgen slams the car door shut behind me. "Let's get to the office so I can see what you and your co-workers came up with."

She leans closer to me. "You're about to be blown away."

———

TWO HOURS LATER, I close the door to the conference room when Delora leaves.

I don't need to face my brother to know how he feels about what just happened.

He was mesmerized as Delora presented details on how the subscription model would work. She also laid out a host of innovative marketing ideas and some creative approaches to using our current social media followers to bump up interest in this campaign.

"This is a fucking winner," Declan says.

I spin around to see a broad smile on his face. "I agree."

"We need to hit the ground running with this today." He taps his left index finger against his right palm. "I want this in place for the holidays. We're running against the clock on this, but we can get it done. Authorize all overtime. Give the marketing department whatever they need to make this a reality."

"Done," I tell him with a brisk nod.

"Do we know who came up with the original idea?" He tilts his head. "Was it Justin? He's been reliably creating solid campaigns since I hired him."

I shake my head. "It was Calliope."

"Callie?" His brows perk. "This is impressive, Sean."

"She's brilliant." I shove my hands into the front pockets of my pants. "Calliope saw the potential in this and presented it to Delora. She passed on it the first time."

"Delora passed on this idea?" Surprise edges his tone.

I nod.

"I'm glad it was put back on the table. This will increase our revenue and it's going to introduce our products to a hell of a lot more people."

"That it will."

"You're proud of her, aren't you?" He steps closer. "I can see it on your face."

"I'm damn proud of Calliope," I say without hesitation. "She works two jobs, helps out her sister with her kids, comes up with killer campaigns for us, and is cooking dinner for a bunch of our neighbors tomorrow night. The woman is a force to be reckoned with."

"If I didn't have plans tomorrow night, I'd invite myself to this dinner."

"Cancel the plans." I point a finger at him. "I'd love for you to be there."

"I would if I could." He glances at the windows that overlook lower Manhattan. "I'm meeting with a representative from Berdine. I've wanted our products in their stores for years."

I know he has. Striking a deal with the menswear retailer would be a coup for Declan.

His gaze lands on me again. "She's good for you, Sean."

"She's too good for me," I say.

"That's where you're wrong." He moves so he can rest a hand on my shoulder. "I've never known a better man than you. You deserve the best in life. Never doubt that."

I pull him in for a quick embrace. It's something we rarely do and have never done at work. "Thanks, Dicky."

Laughing, he steps back. "Decky."

I flash him a smile. "That's what I said."

CHAPTER FORTY-SIX

Callie

I RAP my knuckles against the door, hoping that he'll answer immediately.

A glance down at the watch on my wrist confirms that it's way too late to be bothering anyone, but I have a feeling that the handsome, well-hung man that lives here won't care that I'm waking him up.

I press my ear against the door but am greeted with dead silence.

I huff out a combination sigh and frustrated as fuck noise.

All of this is fueled by the two glasses of wine I had at our celebratory dinner tonight.

Delora got the good news about the subscription model proposal right before quitting time. Thankfully, she already had a reservation at her favorite French restaurant, so we headed straight there. Justin and Rory met us there thirty minutes later, and we all spent the next six hours eating, talking, drinking, and planning.

I did go straight home afterward, but then I had a brilliant idea.

I changed into the pink silk robe I'm wearing now, put on my highest heels, and wandered into the corridor to thank my neighbor for his faith in my idea.

"Saint," I whisper because I don't want to risk waking up Mrs. Sweeney. "Saint, open the door."

I follow that up with another round of knocking.

Finally, I hear a shuffling noise before his door swings open.

"Wowza!" I try to level my breathing. "Are you for real?"

Sean shoots me a grin. "What do we have here?"

My gaze wanders over his bare chest and stomach until it lands on his boxer briefs. They're the same as the pair he's wearing in the image on the billboard in Times Square.

"This is what women in this city dream about," I murmur.

His hand trails over his smooth skin until it reaches his navel. "This right here?"

I circle my hand in front of him. "All of that right there."

"You're blushing," he points out. "Big time blushing."

"You do that to me, " I accuse. "I blush because of you."

He leans his bicep against the doorjamb. "Are you here for all of this right here, or…"

I rehearsed this on my way home, so I might as well put it to good use. "I'd like to borrow a cup of sugar."

That sends his head back in laughter. "Touché."

I poke a finger in the center of his very hard chest. "You always knocked on my door to borrow sugar, so…"

My finger is wrapped in his fist before I realize what's happening. "I was always knocking on your door to look at you."

"Really?"

"Really." He tugs on my hand. "I still owe you some orgasms. Are you here to collect?"

"Am I?" I ask with a tilt of my head.

His response is a yank on my hand to draw me into his home before he slams the door behind me.

———

HE'S PINNED me against the door to his apartment. The only barrier between my nipples and the cool wood is the bra I have on. My robe hit the floor the moment Sean tore it off of me.

"Calliope." That comes out wrapped in a mangled groan. "You're exquisite."

I can feel how hard he is as he presses into me from behind. "Take me like this."

"Like. This," he repeats my words slowly with more meaning than they ever should possess. They sound sensual, and there's a depth of longing in them that is palpable.

"Tell me how that would feel," he teases me with a lick of his tongue up the side of my neck.

Jesus.

I'm glad I pinned up my hair today because that sent a shiver down my spine.

"Like perfection," I squeak out in a moan. "You'd rip my panties off and slide into me."

"Bare?" He growls. "You want my cock in that tight little pussy without anything between us?"

I can't form the single word that would give that to me. I can't say *yes* because it's stuck somewhere inside of me, buried beneath both fear and need.

He doesn't wait for me to respond. He lets his fingers do all the talking, giving…everything.

They slide over the lace of my bra to find my left nipple.

He tweaks it with a sharp pinch as his lips press into the skin below my ear. "I fucking love your nipples. So pretty, so hard, so responsive."

Another tweak and I'm a moaning mess.

I push my ass back, trying to gain more friction against the thick length of his cock. It's still tucked inside his boxer briefs.

"Fuck me," I purr. "I want it now."

"You're so impatient." He follows that up with another pinch to my already sensitive nipple. "I'm going to slowly torture you until you come so hard."

"Promise?" I suck in a deep breath.

It's useless. I can't breathe or think. I can't do anything but chase the orgasm he's holding just out of my reach.

My hand snakes down my body. "I need to come."

His hand finds mine, holding it on my stomach just above the lace waistband of my panties. "Not yet."

"Now," I demand.

He abandons my hand, and in one effortless motion, his hand is inside of my panties. He traces my cleft with a fingertip before touching my clit with the softest stroke.

My head falls back against his shoulder. "Sean, please."

"Shhh." He showers my cheek with soft kisses. "Let go and feel. Just feel."

With my hands pressed against the door, I give in and do as he says.

I feel.

I feel every skilled movement of his hand. I feel his lips against my cheek, and I feel the orgasm race through me before I almost crumble to my knees from the depth of the pleasure of his touch.

CHAPTER FORTY-SEVEN

SEAN

I KNOCK three times on Calliope's door.

I'm fucking late for the dinner she's worked so hard to prepare.

My brother had to bail on a last-minute late-day meeting because of his commitment to meet with the rep from Berdine.

I handled that as quickly as possible, but it still set me back an hour.

I breathe a sigh of relief when Champ swings open the door.

An instant smile pops onto her lips. "You're here!"

"I'm sorry," I say. "Work was a bastard."

"No sorries," she summons me inside with a flick of her wrist. "We haven't sat down to dinner yet."

I shove a wicker basket filled with a half dozen Bosc pears at her. "This is for you."

Her gaze falls to it as I brush past her.

I've never been inside this apartment, but the layout mirrors Mrs. Sweeney's place. That's where the similarities end.

A dark brown leather sofa sits in the center of the open space. To its right is the dining room. There's a mid-size table with a bunch of chairs gathered around it. Some match. Some don't.

One wall is decorated with scattered pictures of people. The frames all vary in style and color, yet they somehow match perfectly with each other.

My gaze travels over those until it reaches the wall that houses a large window. Next to it are four large black frames. Each contains a stunning photograph of New York City taken at night.

Mr. Durkman must agree with me because he's studying them.

"I make a pitcher of sangria," Calliope says. "Do you want some?"

I've never been able to stomach it, but if she crafted it, I know I'll love it. "Please."

"You know everyone." Her hand sweeps across the room. "Get to mingling, Saint."

Before I let her rush off, I subtly link one of my pinkie fingers around one of hers. "Have I told you today how beautiful you are?"

Her gaze drops to the jeans and pink sweater she's wearing. "No, but I'll take the compliment."

"Take it." I tug her hand closer. "Keep it."

That sends her off toward the kitchen with a giggle.

I make my way around the room, stopping to offer my greetings to everyone there. Cornell takes the opportunity to ask a question related to work. As I answer, I catch sight of Champ on the approach with a smile on her face.

My chest feels like it's caving in from happiness.

If this is love, I never again want to feel what I felt the moment before I met her.

"Here you go." She grabs my hand to place a glass tumbler in it. "I made spaghetti, my mom's super secret meat sauce, garlic bread, and a big salad."

Cornell rubs his stomach through the T-shirt he's wearing. "It sounds delicious, Callie. Lee loves spaghetti."

Her gaze darts to where the little boy is playing on the floor with a few wooden blocks. "I found a booster seat in the hall closet. Grady has it for when my niece comes over. We can set that up so Lee can sit at the table with us."

I stare at her. How can one person radiate so much goodness?

"Callie," Mr. Durkman calls out her name. "Tell me where these came from."

She walks over to where he's standing a few feet from us. "The photographs?"

He nods, tapping a finger against the corner of one of the frames. "This one in particular. I took my love to this restaurant on our first date many years ago. It shut down a few months ago, so we don't have anything but our memories. I need a print of this for our apartment."

I scan the photograph. It's of a diner that anchored a corner on Broadway. The word '*restaurant*' is glowing neon red in the image against the rain that is falling. The reflection of the building on the puddled rain on the street only adds to the allure of the image.

"I gave those pictures to Grady as a housewarming gift. I'll get a print to you tomorrow," Calliope says. "I know someone who can frame it for you. They're very affordable. They frame all of my photographs."

The question I'm primed to ask leaves Durkman's lips

before I can get it out. "Your photograph? Did you take this picture, Callie?"

She nods. "I took all of them."

Silence settles over the apartment as the other guests listen in.

Mrs. Sweeney is the first to pipe up. "You're a brilliant photographer, Calliope. The one of the Empire State Building with the full moon as its backdrop is simply beautiful."

"I can get you a print of that one if you'd like."

"I'd like that very much," Mrs. Sweeney responds to Champ. "How much, dear?"

A bubble of laughter escapes Calliope. "No charge. They are only a few dollars."

"If you handle arranging framing of the one I want and you sign it, I'll pay five hundred," Mr. Durkman injects himself back into the conversation.

"Five hundred dollars?" Champ shakes her head. "No. I can't accept that."

"I'll pay a thousand for mine." Mrs. Sweeney one-ups our neighbor. "I've paid twice that for some of the photographs in my apartment. Not one is as beautiful as that one."

Calliope's gaze jumps to my face. I see something that I can only label as shock there.

I'd outbid everyone and offer one hundred thousand for the lot, but that would tarnish this moment for her.

Her bottom lip quivers as she glances at Mrs. Sweeney. "I can't accept that much."

"You can and you will," she insists. "There's a beautiful little tea store that my grandmother used to own. It's in Brooklyn. Multi-colored lights rim the windowsills. It's a dream to see in the evening when the sun is about to set. I'd love a photograph like that. It would be a treasure. Can I commission that?"

Calliope swallows hard. "I would love to take a picture like that for you, but I don't have a camera right now."

"That's a shame." Mrs. Sweeney's hand darts to her chest. "Did your camera break, dear?"

She shakes her head slightly. "I sold it."

That admission slays me. I drop my head because I've witnessed how hard she works. There's no doubt in my mind that she sold that camera because she needed the money. She needed it for her goal.

Freedom. That one word has haunted me since she first said it.

An alarm sounds in the distance. Calliope glances toward the kitchen. "The garlic bread is done. I need to get that out of the oven before it burns."

I reach for her shaking hand. "I'll help."

She squeezes my fingers. "I just need a minute to catch my breath."

"Of course," I whisper.

I stand in place watching her walk away, wishing I could chase after her, gather her into my arms, and never let her go.

CHAPTER FORTY-EIGHT

Callie

I TURN after closing my apartment door to find Sean in front of my photographs. This is our first moment alone since he arrived at my apartment.

"I didn't get a chance to thank you for the basket of pears."

That turns him around to face me. "They're your favorite. I'm hoping that I can feed you pieces of one later."

I start walking toward him. "I think that can be arranged."

The corners of his lips twitch, but they fall before he can form a smile. I know something is bothering him.

He was talkative during dinner, but his witty comebacks weren't present.

At first, I thought his mood might be related to work, but he kept looking at my photographs. I regretted the admission about selling my camera as soon as it left my mouth, but by then, the secret was out.

"What's wrong?" I whisper as I near him.

"Champ," he says my name wrapped in a sigh. "Let me buy you a camera."

"No," I respond without giving it a second of thought. "I'll buy a used one when I can."

"Please."

Shaking my head, I step forward until the toes of our shoes are touching. "When I can afford to buy a camera, I will."

His gaze falls to the floor. "I'm in a position to help you."

I know that he is, but that's a slippery slope that I can't slide down again.

I let Dagen '*help*' me, and it's turned into the biggest mistake of my life.

"I don't need help." I wrap my arms around him, tucking my hands under his suit jacket so I can caress his back. "I need something else."

He runs a fingertip over my chin to lure my head up. With his eyes pinned to mine, he smiles. "Name it. I'll do it."

"Come to bed with me. " I bounce up to my tiptoes to offer my lips to him.

He responds with a slow, sensual kiss that steals every thought from my mind. "I'll never say no to that."

―――

HOURS LATER, I crawl out of bed to find Sean wearing only boxer briefs.

He's on the couch with his phone cradled in his hands.

I stop for a moment to admire him. It's not just the sharp cut of his jaw or the depth of his brown eyes that makes him so utterly irresistible. It's his heart. He offered to buy me a camera without a second thought.

I know that he did that because he cares for me.

He must sense I'm behind him because his gaze suddenly shoots over his shoulder.

He smiles when he spots me standing barefoot in my pink robe. "There she is."

I hurry so I can snuggle in beside him. Once I do, he tugs me closer, so my legs are resting on his lap. He circles a fingertip over my knee. "Did you have fun tonight, Champ?"

Resting my head against his shoulder, I nod. "I did. How about you?"

"I had fun during dinner," he admits. "What we did after was out of this world."

I let out a laugh. "I agree with that."

His hand skims over my thigh. "Delora is hell-bent on keeping you busy this week, and I've got to pick up some slack since Declan is working on a big deal. I'm booked solid for the next two days."

Sighing, I drop my hand to cover his. "I can sneak into your office to say hi."

His responding laugh shakes his chest. "How about I bring in lunch for us on Friday? Can you meet me in my office at one?"

"I think I remember where that is," I tease.

"You remember." He pushes a strand of my hair behind my ear. "I'd also like to cook dinner for you on Saturday if you're free."

"If Delora lets me have the day off, I'll agree to that."

"She'll let you have the day off," he says with a chuckle. "You're doing great things at Wells, Calliope. We're damn lucky to have you."

I lean back so I can gaze into his eyes. "Thank you, Saint."

His hand jumps up to cradle my cheek. "I'm damn lucky to have you."

"I'm lucky too," I whisper before pressing my lips to his.

I kiss him tenderly, and with every beat of my heart, I'm falling more in love with him.

CHAPTER FORTY-NINE

Callie

BEFORE I ENTER Sean's office, I already know what he ordered us for lunch. I'd recognize the aroma of my favorite fish tacos anywhere.

I take another two steps forward until I'm standing near the open doorjamb.

My hand skims over the front of the black jeans I'm wearing. I chose a white blouse and a red blazer to go with the jeans since Delora announced yesterday that she had made an executive decision to make today casual Friday.

I was all in since I feel like I'm running on empty. I've put in extra hours all week, and I picked up a late shift at Tin Anchor last night. I started that at nine and left the bar around two this morning.

I fell asleep the moment my head hit my pillow.

Hopefully, I can catch up on sleep tonight, so I'm well rested for my date with Sean tomorrow.

I take the final step that brings me into the open doorjamb.

I spot Sean sitting behind his desk, but his back is turned to me. Since he left for the office before I did this morning, I haven't had a chance to see him yet today.

"Excuse me?" I say softly. "I have a one o'clock meeting with Mr. Wells."

I said the very same words not more than three minutes ago when I approached Sean's assistant. He smiled and told me that his boss was expecting me and then congratulated me on my work on the upcoming campaign.

It felt good to be acknowledged for all the effort that I'm putting in.

Sean spins around in his chair. An instant smile coasts over his lips. "Calliope."

He's up and out of his chair before I take another step forward.

Looking sexy as sin in a tailored dark blue suit and green striped tie, I stare at him. "Sean."

"Are you hungry?" he asks as he moves past me to shut the door. "I hope you are. I ordered in a few of your favorites."

My gaze falls to his desk and the many take-out containers. There are fish tacos, chips and salsa, fresh cut fruit, and a plate of rice cereal treats off to the side. To wash it all down, there are two cans of soda and a couple of bottles of water.

"This is incredibly thoughtful," I whisper.

He moves to stand next to me. "I've missed you, Champ."

I look up and into his eyes. I see calmness, confidence, and compassion there. I've never had anyone put in this much effort just for me.

"I've missed you," I say.

His hands leap to my cheeks. "I could barely sleep last night. I was so excited for this lunch."

I let out a small laugh. "Seriously?"

His lips find mine for a tender, sweet kiss. "Seriously, Calliope. If I haven't already told you, I'm falling for you."

Those words mean everything to me. I no longer feel scared by the thought of falling in love again. I only feel joy and a sense of peace I've never felt before.

I belong with him. I belong in his arms, in his life. I belong in this wonderful man's world.

I kiss him, but this time it's deeper. It lingers, and when our lips part, he breathes out a sigh. "That puts every other kiss in the history of kisses to shame."

Running a fingertip over his bottom lip, I smile. "We will do that again after we eat."

He gazes into my eyes. "I hope you have a huge appetite because I ordered extra."

"I'm starving." I move toward one of the chairs that face his desk. "I can't wait to eat."

―――

I LEAN BACK in my chair and watch Sean as he takes a business call. After his desk phone rang the first time, he called his assistant to remind him that he had been instructed to hold all calls.

I could tell by the shift in Sean's expression that something needed his immediate attention. He confirmed that when he told me he needed to return the missed call but wanted me to stay put.

He handles whoever is on the other end with ease, even though I can hear that they have raised their voice. The phone may be pressed to Sean's ear, but the volume of the caller's voice is loud enough that I can catch bits and pieces of what he's saying.

Not wanting to full on eavesdrop, I glance around Sean's office.

The first time I was here, I was too nervous to notice any small details. I was completely focused on the man sitting behind the desk because I had called the police on him just hours earlier.

My gaze catches on a series of framed photographs sitting atop a shelf near the window. I push back from my chair to get a better look.

As I make my way toward them, I glance at Sean to find his gaze pinned to me. A slow smile slides over his lips.

I know that look.

If he weren't in the middle of a heated business discussion, I imagine he'd have me pinned to the wall or spread out on his desk with his head between my legs.

I shake off that thought because I don't want to have to explain why I'm blushing.

I turn my attention to the framed photographs. One is of Sean and Declan. They look a few years younger than they are now. I can tell that they're in an office. It's much smaller than anything I've seen in this building but behind them is a cardboard sign with their surname scribbled across it in black marker.

The picture next to it is of a couple with two boys standing in front of them. The woman in the photo is cradling a baby in her arms. I pick up the frame to get a closer look, and I instantly recognize the taller of the two boys. It's Declan. The other one has to be Sean. He can't be more than nine or ten years old.

In the third photo, Sean's older but only by a few years. His hair is longer. He's sporting some sparse facial hair, and his T-shirt is stamped with the logo from a fast food place. He's with three other young men who look to be the same age as he is. If pressed to guess, I'd peg them at sixteen or seventeen.

"Take an hour to consider what I just said." Sean's voice catches my attention. "Then call me back."

With that, he ends the call.

"That seemed to go well," I tease.

Laughing, he pushes to his feet, buttoning his suit jacket. "It's all in a day's work."

I glance back at the photos. "How old were you in this picture?"

He closes the distance between us with a few measured steps. "Sixteen. That was taken at the boarding school I went to. Those guys are my three closest friends."

I stare into his face, noticing the soft smile. "What are their names?"

He taps a finger against the glass of the frame. "That's Graham, next to him is Harrison, and on the end is Kavan."

Kavan.

I've heard that name before.

Without thinking, I blurt out, "Kavan Bane?"

"That's right." Sean turns toward me. "You've heard of him?"

Dagen told me that Kavan killed his father. He made a point of telling me that he had been a friend to Kavan at one time since they went to the same boarding school and shared some classes. More recently, I read about Kavan in a column written by his fiancée. It was a love letter to him by Juliet Bardin that appeared in a magazine called New York Viewpoint.

"I read about him," I admit softly. "In New York Viewpoint."

"Right." He nods. "Juliet, his fiancée, wrote that. She did a damn fine job."

I swallow past the lump in my throat as I stare into the eyes of the man I'm head over heels in love with. "You went to The Buchanan School, didn't you?"

"I did." He beams. "I'm a Buck Boy through and through."

I've heard those exact words before, but they came from the mouth of a different man. It was the man I was supposed to marry.

My gaze drops to the floor. "I should get back to work."

Sean's desk phone starts ringing just as I feel the tender touch of his fingers against mine. "I should too, Champ. I'll see you for dinner tomorrow night."

I don't answer because he's turned around and headed back to his desk.

Instead, I quietly sneak out in search of the nearest washroom, so I can take a moment alone to catch my breath before I head back to my desk.

CHAPTER FIFTY

Sean

I WALK into the foyer of my parents' townhouse on Saturday morning to another unlikely Declan sighting. This time he's sporting a pair of board shorts that he must have last worn a decade ago.

"What the hell?" I spit the words out through a laugh. "This fashion show you're putting on for me needs to stop. Those are too damn tight."

He reaches down to cup the front of the shorts. "I should have been on that billboard, Saint. Just admit it."

I haven't seen my brother shirtless in years, but *dammit,* it's possible he may be in better shape than I am.

In addition to the tattoo that's graced his chest since he was a teenager, he now has one that runs down his side. It looks like something written in script that I can't quite make out.

"You wouldn't have agreed to be on the billboard," I point

out. "Something about you being a lawyer and being too distinguished for that."

His head falls back as he chuckles. "Law is still my backup plan."

It was his first and only plan until I approached him with the idea of launching an underwear brand. Declan gave up a promising law career to jump into the business with me. He didn't have to do it, but he knew how much I wanted to be my own boss, so he put the career he worked hard for on hold to be by my side.

I owe him everything, and there's no way I can repay him.

"Put on some pants," I say as I brush past him, holding a cup of coffee in each hand. "The board shorts need to go into the donation pile."

"No chance in hell."

I steal a glance at him over my shoulder. "What time did you get here?"

"I slept here last night."

That turns me back around to stare at him. "You what?"

"The alarm went off around midnight," he explains. "Mom called me in a panic, so I came down to check it out."

I glance around, noting that everything looks in order, including the vases my mother covets and the paintings on the wall that she has deemed priceless.

"By the time I got here, the police were waiting out front." He laughs. "There was a patrol car in the area, so they stopped by to check it out after the alarm company called it in."

"Let me guess," I begin before taking a sip from one of the coffee cups. "You called mom back to tell her all that, and she asked you to watch guard just in case the bad guy came back."

His left brow perks. "No. I came inside to check on things

and sat down for a minute, and lights out. I fell asleep on the couch."

I shove a cup of coffee at him. "I've slept on the couch. It's hard as hell. You must be exhausted."

He takes a long drink from the coffee. "It was wild being back in this place for the night. It's full of memories. Good and bad."

I glance around the room we're standing in. It's where our mother sets up the Christmas tree each year. We'd gather here for our monthly family meetings, which were just an excuse for our parents to get us all together in one place as we grew older.

"Mostly good memories," I add. "We were lucky growing up in this place, Decky."

"Damn lucky," he agrees. "Do you see yourself in a house like this when you settle down?"

Before I met Calliope, I wouldn't have entertained the idea of settling down, but that's changed now. I can see a future with her. I can imagine special occasions being by her side and carrying her over the threshold of a home chosen by the two of us.

"I can see it," I say. "I can finally see it."

"With Callie?" he asks tentatively.

I nod. "Yes."

Keeping his gaze trained on my face, he steps closer to me. "Are you in love with her, Sean?"

"Yeah," I admit. "I am."

He closes the distance between us to pat me on the cheek. "I'm happy for you. You deserve it more than anyone."

"I don't deserve her." I smile. "She's too good for me, but don't tell her that."

DECLAN and I take the same path I took the night when I stumbled on Calliope standing outside the building we're approaching now. We're on the hunt for something to eat.

I insisted we come this way so I could drop off something for Leon. I may not know the guy, but he's a friend to Champ, so that's all that matters to me.

"There's a deli two blocks from here. We can grab some sandwiches to take back to my apartment," Declan says from behind me. "We'll eat, I'll shower, and then we can go into the office for a couple of hours. We need to catch up on a few things before Monday."

He's lagging because he's been texting one of our district managers non-stop since we left the townhouse. I got the initial text but passed it on to my brother because he'll handle the issue while I stop to talk to Leon.

"Sounds good," I call back to him. "Lunch is my treat this time."

I slow as I near the building where Calliope used to live.

"This is it?" Declan asks as he takes the spot next to me. "You're giving the pen to someone here?"

The pen in question is any pen collector's dream. It's silver and ornate with a designer brand name stamped along its side. The case we found it in bears the same brand name.

The forgotten pen was a gift from one of my uncles when I graduated middle school. He had just returned from a trip to Bali, where he bought it.

I was a teenage kid with no use for a silver pen since I received it right at the start of summer vacation. It ended up abandoned in a box with a bunch of comic books, a few packages of stale bubble gum, and a poster of my favorite skateboarder.

I imagine the pen is worth a few hundred dollars, but it's

not something I'll use. It'll bring more joy to Leon since it sounds like something he'll covet.

"One of the doormen," I say as I peek inside the bank of windows at the front of the building. "I'll check to see if he's on shift. If he's not, I'll try another run at him next week."

"I'll wait here." Declan points at his shiny black shoes.

He switched out the board shorts for the suit he was wearing yesterday. I'm weekend casual in jeans and a black sweater. I may be following his lead to the office today, but there's no one there to impress.

"Be right back," I toss out before I approach the double glass doors of the building that Calliope once called home.

I spot Leon immediately. He's behind a reception desk tucked away near the elevators. There's a cap on his head and his uniform looks freshly pressed.

"Leon!" I call out to him.

He turns to glance in my direction. His gaze wanders my face as I approach him as if he's trying to place me.

"Sean Wells," I help him out with a gentle reminder. "We met one night when Calliope Morrow stopped by."

His face brightens with a wide-mouthed smile. "Of course. Mr. Wells. It's good to see you, sir. If you're looking for Miss Morrow, she's not here. She only stops by on occasion."

"I'm here to see you." I hold out the rectangular box with the pen. "Calliope said you have a pen collection. I thought you might want to add this one to it."

"Sir?" He glances at the box and then at my face. "What do you have there?"

I snap open the lid, and the guy's eyes widen in their sockets. His jaw drops too. This gift from good old Uncle Bruce is about to make someone happy.

"I've seen pictures of this, but I've never…" He runs a gloved fingertip over the pen. "How much?"

The question catches me off guard. "It's free, Leon. I brought it for you."

"You did?" His eyes search my face. "Why?"

"Why?" I echo. "Why not?"

That draws a hearty round of laughter from the gray-haired man. "You sound like Miss Morrow. She brings me pens just because she knows I collect them."

I shove the pen at him. "Add this one to that collection."

He reaches for the box. "You're sure, sir?"

"Positive." I glance beyond his shoulder to the bank of elevators.

"Can I do anything for you?" he asks quietly. "I feel I should repay you for your kindness."

I could use his gratitude to fuel my curiosity by asking the name of the fool Calliope used to live with, but that feels like a betrayal.

I step back and shake my head. "No need, Leon. Enjoy the pen."

"Thank you again, Mr. Wells. I'm glad Miss Morrow has a friend like you. She deserves only the best."

"You're right about that." I pat him on the shoulder. "Calliope deserves the world."

I turn to leave and make it a few steps before one of the double doors open, and a blond-haired man dressed in a white polo and matching shorts walks in.

He stops mid-step when he catches sight of me.

I stare at him. He's changed slightly since I last saw him, but it's unmistakably the bastard I took to the ground in high school. I still remember what it felt like when my fist connected with his nose.

With a smug look on his face, he approaches me.

"I thought I saw your brother standing outside," he drawls. "Tell me you're not moving in here, Wells."

Tell me you're not the asshole that Calliope was engaged to.

I keep that to myself while I try to process the fact that I'm staring at Dagen Hillstead.

"Mr. Wells isn't moving in," Leon drops his two cents into the middle of this reunion. "He's a friend of Miss Morrow."

Dagen's face morphs from a self-assured dick to a surprised bastard. "You know Callie?"

Struggling to keep my tone even, I look him dead in the eye. "I'm in love with her."

CHAPTER FIFTY-ONE

CALLIE

DON'T PANIC.

I tell myself that for the third time as my gaze drops to the watch on my wrist.

Sean and I agreed to meet for dinner at his place at seven. It's nearing eight thirty now, and he's not home. He also hasn't responded to any of the three texts I've sent him in the past few hours.

The first was at six to see if I could bring anything for our dinner.

I followed that up with another one at seven fifteen, asking if he was asleep since I had knocked on his door, and he didn't answer.

I sent the last one ten minutes ago, telling him I'm worried and hope he's okay.

I also hope that *we* are okay.

My after dinner plans included telling Sean about Dagen.

If Dagen knows Kavan, there's an excellent, almost one hundred percent chance that he knows Sean too.

Part of me is scared that Sean will feel some sort of loyalty to Dagen that will pull him away from me. I know that Dagen felt that with a few of his friends. All of them went to the elite boarding school too.

Feeling as though the walls are closing in on me, I decide to take a walk. I can circle the block a few times and then try Sean again. Maybe, he'll be home by then. I keep telling myself that he's dealing with a work catastrophe.

I can't imagine what that would consist of, but it's the thin thread I'm clinging to right now, and I don't want to let it go.

I grab my phone and keys and head out the door.

I'm still wearing the blue lace sundress I put on for dinner. Earlier today, I found it at the vintage store I love. Wearing it with my white blazer will transform it into office attire. It's too warm for that tonight, so I've paired it with flat sandals.

As I check to make sure that my apartment door is locked, I hear a soft noise behind me.

Startled, I turn abruptly.

The door to Mrs. Sweeney's apartment is opening very slowly. It's almost as if time has crept to slow motion.

Finally, she peeks her head out. "This is fate."

I approach her. "What is fate?"

"I was just about to cross the hall to see you." Her hand pops into view with her index finger raised. "Give me a moment, Calliope."

I steal a glance at the door to Saint's apartment. I'm tempted to go and knock on it again, but I know he's not in there. I can't imagine Sean intentionally ignoring me.

I hear the sound of Mrs. Sweeney's sneakers as they hit

the wood in the foyer of her apartment. The door swings open, and she's standing in front of me with a broad smile and a gift-wrapped box in her hands.

"I have something for you, dear."

Taken aback, my hand jumps to the center of my chest. "For me?"

She shoves the box at me. "Open it, Calliope."

Not one to deny a kind woman anything, I tuck my phone and keys into the pockets of my dress and take the box from her. With one swift pull of the ribbon tied around it, the wrapping paper falls to the side, revealing the box of a digital camera.

It's the same brand as the one I sold six months ago, but it's a newer model. It has all the bells and whistles that mine didn't have.

My gaze darts up to Mrs. Sweeney's face. "I can't accept this."

Her kind eyes stare into mine. "Consider it a trade."

"A trade?"

"A fair trade." She smiles. "In exchange for the camera, you'll get that print framed for me and take a photo of my grandmother's tea shop and frame that as well. Does that sound fair to you?"

Not at all.

I shake my head. "This is far too generous. It won't cost me much to frame that print."

"Your time and talent are worth far more than the price of that camera." She pats my forearm. "I went to the camera shop that my grandson works at. He's the one who recommended that particular model. He knows his stuff."

I laugh through sudden tears. "I don't know what to say, Mrs. Sweeney."

"Say that you'll accept it in the spirit it's been given." Her hand lingers on my arm. "Use it to capture this city in all its splendor. Share those pictures with the world. A creative hobby feeds the soul, and if you can make a few extra bucks while pursuing it, more power to you."

This camera feels like a stepping-stone toward my new life.

"Thank you." My voice quivers. "I'm so grateful."

She gathers me into her arms. "I'm going to tell everyone I know that my neighbor takes the most breathtaking photos of our city. I have a feeling that there's going to be a line of people waiting to buy one of your future creations."

CHAPTER FIFTY-TWO

Callie

A QUICK WALK around the block did little to curb the anxiety that is still twisting my gut into knots.

I haven't tried texting or calling Sean again, but I'm about two minutes away from typing out a message asking if he's still alive.

I glance over to where I set the camera Mrs. Sweeney got me.

I had a hard cry after I brought it into my apartment. As I was unpacking it, I had visions of a photography show at the small gallery in midtown. I haven't been able to afford the cost of the opening night of an exhibit of my photographs.

I'd want a catered affair much like Adam had.

Maybe, just maybe, I can set aside some of my tips from Tin Anchor for that.

A soft knock at my door sends my gaze in that direction.

I hope it's Sean, but I suspect it's Mrs. Sweeney. Before I left her at her apartment door, she told me she was in the middle of baking a batch of chocolate chip cookies for Sean. She promised to drop off a half dozen for me to feed my sweet tooth.

I drop my bare feet to the floor and slide off the couch.

As another knock fills the silent space, I up my pace so I can get to the door as quickly as possible.

I swing it open and stare. I just stare up and into the face of the man I love.

My hand darts to my mouth because, *oh my god*, he's sporting a black eye.

"Sean." My voice is breathless, which makes perfect sense since my breath is caught somewhere between my lungs and my lips.

"You should see the other guy," he quips.

"The other guy?" I tilt my head to get a better angle of his eye. "What did you do to him?"

"I broke his nose in high school. "He flashes me a smile. "It's still as crooked as the day it happened."

My brow furrows. "What?"

"You've seen the other guy, Champ. You've seen what I did to his nose."

I slowly piece that together. "You're talking about Dagen, aren't you? You're the guy who broke his nose."

"Guilty as charged." He takes a step closer to me. "I went to drop off a pen for Leon this afternoon. I ran into Hillstead in the lobby. He ran his fist into my face, and we ended up at the police station."

I PLACE a small bag of frozen peas against Sean's eye. "Does this hurt?"

"Damn right it does," he says, tossing his head back until

it's resting on the back of the couch. "I'm sorry I didn't respond to your messages. I didn't notice them until I walked out of the police station. I wanted to have this conversation in person."

This conversation.

I've been hiding my secret for so long that I've never considered having a conversation about it with anyone, especially not the man I've fallen in love with.

"When I saw the picture in your office yesterday, I realized there was a good chance that you knew Dagen," I confess. "I had no idea that you were the guy who broke his nose."

He glances at me with his uninjured eye. "He deserved it."

I nod. "I'm not surprised."

I don't know how to explain how I got so involved with Dagen Hillstead that I was on the cusp of marrying him. It wasn't a whirlwind romance. He didn't sweep me off my feet. Our connection built slowly after he stopped at Tin Anchor one night. He came back repeatedly before I agreed to go out with him.

I believed I was in love with him, but what I felt for him can't compare to what I feel for Sean.

"He deserves worse for what he's put you through. He told me everything, Champ. I know what the bastard is holding over you."

Tears well in my eyes. I hang my head to shield them from him. "I'm so ashamed."

"For what?" The words leave him in a rush. "For trusting a man who claimed to love you? For believing that he wanted what was best for you?"

I look into his face. "For letting my guard down."

He tosses the peas onto the coffee table before moving

closer to me. "You have nothing to be ashamed of. You have worked so damn hard to get out from underneath this burden. I can't tell you how badly I want to fix this for you."

"I have to fix it." I calm him with a hand on his knee. "It's important to me that I fix it. I have to see this through to the end."

"I know." He scoops my hand into his to press a kiss on my palm.

"You said that he told you everything," I whisper. "But that's coming from Dagen's point of view. Can I tell you everything from my point of view?"

He turns so he's facing me head-on. "Tell me, Calliope. Tell me how you ended up owing Dagen Hillstead more than forty thousand dollars."

"It's not that amount anymore. I've chipped away at it since we broke up."

"By working at Tin Anchor?" he asks. "By working two jobs?"

"Yes." I breathe in a heavy sigh. "And by packing my lunch for work. By shopping at vintage shops and by selling things."

"Like your camera?"

I glance at the new camera on the foyer table. "Yes. I sold it and gave that money to him."

Sean reaches for my hand to squeeze. It's a sign of silent encouragement.

I jump back to the beginning of my tale. "I went to college on a small scholarship but needed to take out student loans to pay for the remainder."

I know that Sean doesn't have experience with that or the fact that at times debt can feel like a heavy burden to shoulder.

"When Dagen and I became more serious, he told me that

he wanted to clear that debt to take that worry away." I shake my head. "We never discussed the terms of that. I foolishly assumed it was a gift. Apparently, Dagen viewed it as a loan because when I dumped him…"

"He demanded that money back," Sean interrupts.

"It was his way of keeping me in his world," I tell him. "He brought it up as I was packing my things. I knew at that moment that I'd pay back every penny, so I'd never be connected to him again. Dagen and I had reached a point where my dreams were secondary to his. What I wanted in life didn't matter to him. He didn't think marketing was the career path for me. He hated that I worked as a bartender. He believed that I should give up my dreams to fulfill his. He made it clear that once we were married, he expected me to work for him as his assistant at his consulting firm."

"He's pathetic," Sean murmurs.

"I looked into taking out a loan to clear what I owed him, but I couldn't get approved because my employment situation wasn't stable." I take a deep breath. "Going to my parents or my oldest brother wasn't an option. Everyone had warned me that Dagen wasn't right for me. "

Sean squeezes my hand again. "I understand."

I glance down at our hands. "My sister knew. She suggested I sell my engagement ring to pay off the debt, but it didn't belong to me. I gave it back to Dagen a week after I left him."

"Has he been harassing you, Champ?" Sean gazes into my eyes. "Has he been after you to get it paid off?"

I shrug. "He'll text me to say we should meet up to discuss it, or he'll call and invite me to dinner to renegotiate the terms of the loan even though there are no terms. I've tried to get him to leave me alone, and he will for a few weeks, but inevitably, I always hear from him again. I think he believes there's a chance we'll get back together even though I've told him that will never happen."

Sean leans closer to me. "He doesn't believe that anymore, Calliope."

My gaze searches his face, stalling at the bruised skin around his eye. "How do you know that?"

"I told him I'm in love with you," he whispers. "I told him that one day I intend to marry you, and that means he needs to stay the fuck away from you."

CHAPTER FIFTY-THREE

Sean

I DON'T KNOW if anything will ever spear my heart the way Calliope's tears do.

I just confessed that I love her, and with a trembling bottom lip and tears streaming down her cheeks, she nods and the faintest of words come out of her mouth. "I love you too."

"You love me?" I ask because I'm that guy.

I need to hear it again and again because if it's true, I've just been handed the winning ticket in the life lottery.

Her hand moves to her chest to rest over the lace on the front of her sundress. "With all of my heart."

"Every last piece of it?"

She lets out a laugh. "Yes."

With my heart beating a victory song against my rib cage, I move in for a kiss. It's our first kiss after professing our love for each other, so this will be filed away as one of the most memorable moments of my life.

I take her mouth softly, guiding my tongue over the seam

of her lips until she parts them for me. The kiss is slow, sensual, and will stay with me until the day I die.

Her hands cup my cheeks, holding me there after the kiss breaks. "You said you want to marry me one day."

"Tomorrow works for me."

A soft laugh falls from her lips, her breath skimming over my cheek. "One day, I'd love to marry you."

I won't push because she's mere months from the end of a serious relationship, and even though I know my heart has always been hers, I won't push for anything she's not ready for.

"We'll revisit that when the time feels right for both of us," I suggest.

She moves back slightly so she can see into my eyes. "I'm sorry you got punched today, Saint."

I huff out a laugh. "He wanted to even the score. He got a punch in and a few choice words about me, but in the end, he's still the same guy I knew from high school. Leon was the one who called the police. They took us both in, but ultimately I decided not to press any charges. We don't need that guy in our lives anymore."

"I don't know how I ever thought he was right for me."

I inch her chin up with my fingers. "Don't question yourself. Maybe when you met him, he seemed like the right guy because of who you were at the time. You've matured since then. You've grown. You're this kick ass woman with a better sense of who you are now. The past is the past, Calliope."

She nods.

"Speaking of the past," I carefully broach the subject I've wanted to since I realized she's carrying a burden. "I'm going to put this out there one last time, but I know what you'll say. You're going to…"

"Pay Dagen back on my own," she interrupts. "I have to,

Sean. I know you'd clear that for me today, but I have to do it myself. I hope you understand that."

I do, so I tell her as much. "I get it, Champ."

Her gaze trails from my face to something behind me. "Mrs. Sweeney bought me a camera. It's a trade, actually. The camera for the framed print she likes and another print of her grandmother's tea shop."

I steal a glance over my shoulder to spot a camera box. "That's fantastic."

"One of my dreams was to have a show at the gallery I took you to." Her eyes stare into mine. "If I save some of my tips from the bar, I can afford to frame more of my photographs and have an exhibit opening night that people will flock to."

I see the wheels churning as she envisions what that would be like.

"I think I could sell photographs of my favorite places in the city," she whispers as if she's testing out the validity of the idea. "If I do that, I'll have the debt cleared well before I thought I would."

I still want to pay it off myself, but I won't do that. I can't. I respect her too much to go against what she wants.

"I'll help with that," I offer. "I'll be your photography assistant."

"You'd be my assistant?" She laughs. "How would that work exactly?"

"I'll ride the subway with you to all your shoots." I skim my lips over her cheek in search of the soft flesh of her neck. "I'll help you frame the photographs, and I've got some serious skill when it comes to a hammer and nails, so I'm the ideal guy to help with setting up the exhibit."

She lets out a little moan when my lips reach the base of her neck.

"I'll spread the word about your work," I murmur. "Everyone in this city will know that my future fiancée has an upcoming exhibit."

"The leap from girlfriend to future fiancée happened fast," she says.

"It's never too fast when you know you've met the one for you," I tell her as I circle the tip of my tongue on her collarbone. "You're the one for me, Champ."

"You're the one for me." The words come out wrapped in a purr. "You're my forever, Saint."

"You are my forever," I say clearly and passionately, as I continue my path down her body. "My always and forever."

EPILOGUE

3 Months Later

SEAN

I DON'T KNOW if fate or luck's light is shining on me tonight, but everything is lined up as straight as an arrow.

I've been planning this night for weeks.

Not only is it opening night for Calliope's photography exhibition, but it's also the night I pop the question to the love of my life.

I've been holding off on doing that because I promised myself I'd give her time to work on the exhibit without my romantic dreams getting in the way of that.

Champ took her time creating an exhibit that featured photographs that held a special significance to the two of us.

I didn't realize that until I walked into the gallery three hours ago and spotted an image taken from the roof of our building. It showcased the grandeur of Manhattan at night with endless lights in the distance.

Judging from the angle that the photograph was taken, Calliope got closer to the edge than she ever has before.

Next to that photograph was one of the exterior of this gallery, along with another of the taco truck that Barney owns. When my gaze landed on a shot of the outside of our building with Lester standing guard by the door, I almost lost it.

I had my wallet out, ready to buy the entire lot of pictures, but Champ whispered in my ear that there would be prints of all of them hanging in our home by the end of the night.

Her brother, Grady, is seeing to that.

The day before he returned to Manhattan, I helped Calliope carry her things over to my place. I didn't have to ask her to move in. We both knew it would happen. It was understood. That's how our connection works.

It was the same way during her last shift at Tin Anchor. That happened two nights ago. Even though she didn't ask me to be there, I arrived before her and sat at my regular seat at the end of the bar. The smile I received when she spotted me said it all. She was thrilled I was there to see her through to the end of that chapter of her life.

She was just as tickled pink when I went with her to the hospital the day her newest nephew was born. We arrived with a large stuffed blue elephant for Naomi and Harlan's son, Bowie.

I approach where Calliope is standing next to Graham and Trina. Little Sela is bundled in a blanket in Graham's arms. She was passed around to Kavan, his wife, and Harrison earlier. I took a turn holding the little pink-clothed bundle of joy too.

I swear to fuck, she smiled at me, but Graham told me that it was gas.

I highly doubt that. I know I'm the kids' favorite uncle even though she was the star guest of honor at Kavan and Juliet's wedding. There are dozens of pictures documenting that baby girl's adventures so far.

Calliope and I plan on having a couple of kids one day, although that's not in our near future. We ditched the condoms, but she's still on birth control. Loving each other is all that we have planned for now.

"Your talent knows no bounds, Callie," Trina Locke says. "I'm so thrilled that we were able to grab one of the photographs before you sold out."

Calliope nods. "Thank you for that."

"No, thank you," Graham interjects. "We've already picked out a spot for it in our home."

Champ glances at me, and almost instantly her cheeks blush pink. "Hey."

"Hey," I repeat back. "It's about time to shut this party down."

Our agreement with the gallery was to clear out by midnight. Tomorrow, I'll help Calliope package all the photographs that sold tonight for delivery, and we'll display a host of new ones. The space is hers for a month.

"I'm ready to go home," she says. "Are you?"

"I'm ready."

I'm ready to take her home and drop to one knee to ask her to spend the rest of her life with me.

―――

"I'M SO FUCKING EXCITED about the winter campaign." Calliope shoots me a look as we ride the elevator up to our floor. "Tonight, Delora told me that Decky approved the print ads and the new billboard concept for Times Square."

That bastard.

I wanted to be the one to put that smile on her face. Of course, my brother would step into the role of superhero before I had the chance.

He also bought up one of Champ's photos tonight and commissioned one of our parents' townhouse as an anniversary gift for them.

When I told him I was popping the question, he promised me that he'd be the best brother-in-law in town. He's already living up to that.

"I approved them too," I say as we step off the lift on our floor.

"I know." She shoots me a look. "A new model each month will grab a lot more attention, not that your half-naked body hasn't accomplished that."

I let out a low chuckle.

She shoots me a smile. "I'm just thrilled that my idea took root, and soon I'll see it all come to fruition."

I stop her from stepping forward by grabbing hold of her elbow. "I'm proud of you. I'm so damn proud of you."

"Thank you," she whispers. "I didn't want to say anything in front of anyone else, but with the sales tonight and the promised commissions for custom photos, I'm free, Sean."

Her ex hasn't tried to reach out since our altercation in the lobby of his building. That's been a relief for my love, but having that debt in her rear view mirror finally puts her past to rest forever.

I swallow back a rush of emotion. "Let's take this to the roof to celebrate."

Her gaze drops to one of the pockets of the suit jacket I'm

wearing. I went with a dark blue three-piece to compliment the light blue dress she's wearing.

She takes a half-step closer to me. Her bottom lip quivers before she digs her top teeth into it to still it. "Are you going to ask me to marry you tonight?"

I see no reason to lie, so I nod. "I am."

"I'm going to say yes," she whispers.

In that case, why waste another goddamn minute?

I drop to one knee and tug the ring box out of my pocket. I pop open the lid. I picked up the ring the day after we passed the window of a jewelry store called Whispers of Grace in SoHo. Calliope stared at the one-of-kind custom ring. The very next day, I went back and scooped it up. The designer and owner of the store, Ivy Walker-Marlow, told me how she'd come to envision the unique design that includes a circle of small pink diamonds around the larger stone in the center. The glow of the sunset as it enveloped the city inspired her. That was all I needed to hear to know this ring was created for my love.

Calliope lets out the tiniest gasp.

I stare up and into her eyes. "Before we met, I thought my life was complete, but then you charged into it. You are the strongest person I've ever met. Your fearlessness knows no bounds. You taught me how to love, cherish, and trust in someone. I will do everything within my power to be the partner you deserve. I will stand by your side and be blown away each and every day by your beauty and your capacity to love."

"I love you," she whispers. "I love you so much."

"Marry me, Calliope. Honor me by becoming my wife, and I vow never to let you down. I will do everything in my power to make you the happiest woman on this earth, and I will love you until I die."

"I will." She holds out her left hand. "I will marry you."

I slide the ring on her finger, stand, and scoop the woman of my dreams into my arms.

The kiss I plant on her mouth is one for the ages, and as we slowly part, she looks into my eyes. "Do you think Mrs. Sweeney is watching us through her peephole?"

"You know she is," I whisper. "Let's head inside because what I want to do to you next is for our eyes only."

As I unlock the door to our apartment, she holds tightly to my hand. "We are going to have the most amazing life, Saint."

I turn to look at her. "We already are, Champ. We're just getting started."

ALSO BY DEBORAH BLADON
& SUGGESTED READING ORDER

The Obsessed Series

The Exposed Series

The Pulse Series

Impulse

The Vain Series

Solo

The Ruin Series

The Gone Series

Fuse

The Trace Series

Chance

The Ember Series

The Rise Series

Haze

Shiver

Torn

The Heat Series

Risk

melt

The Tense Duet

Sweat

Troublemaker

Worth

Hush

Bare

Wish

Sin

Lace

Thirst

Compass

Versus

Ruthless

Bloom

Rush

Catch

Frostbite

Xoxo

He Loves Me Not

Bittersweet

The Blush Factor

BULL

CRUEL

Starlight

THANK YOU

Thank you for purchasing and downloading my book. I can't even begin to put to words what it means to me. If you enjoyed it, please remember to write a review for it. Let me know your thoughts! I want to keep my readers happy.

For more information on new series and standalones, please visit my website, deborahbladon.com. There are book trailers and other goodies to check out.

Feel free to reach out to me! I love connecting with all of my readers because without you, none of this would be possible.

Thank you, for everything.

ABOUT THE AUTHOR

Deborah Bladon has never read a romance hero she didn't like. Her love for romance novels began when she was old enough to board the bus, library card in hand to check out the newest Harlequin paperbacks. She's a Canadian by heart, and by passport, but you can often spot her in New York City sipping a latte and looking for inspiration for her next story. Manhattan is definitely her second home.

She cherishes her family and believes that each day is a gift for writing, for reading, and for loving.

Printed in Great Britain
by Amazon